Asante's Gullah Journey

~Library Soul Series 1~

S. A. Gibson

Asante's Gullah Journey

ISBN: 1537010263
ISBN-13: 978-1537010267

The cover artwork was provided
especially for this book by
Aaron Radney.

Cover design and layout
by Rachel Bostwick.

DEDICATIONS

Devoted to Charlotte Gibson and the friends and family who made it possible to find the time and space for this series.

Thanks to EJ Runyon for development editing assistance.

Thanks to the Facebook group *The Dragon's Rocketship* for advice and encouragement.

Table of CONTENTS

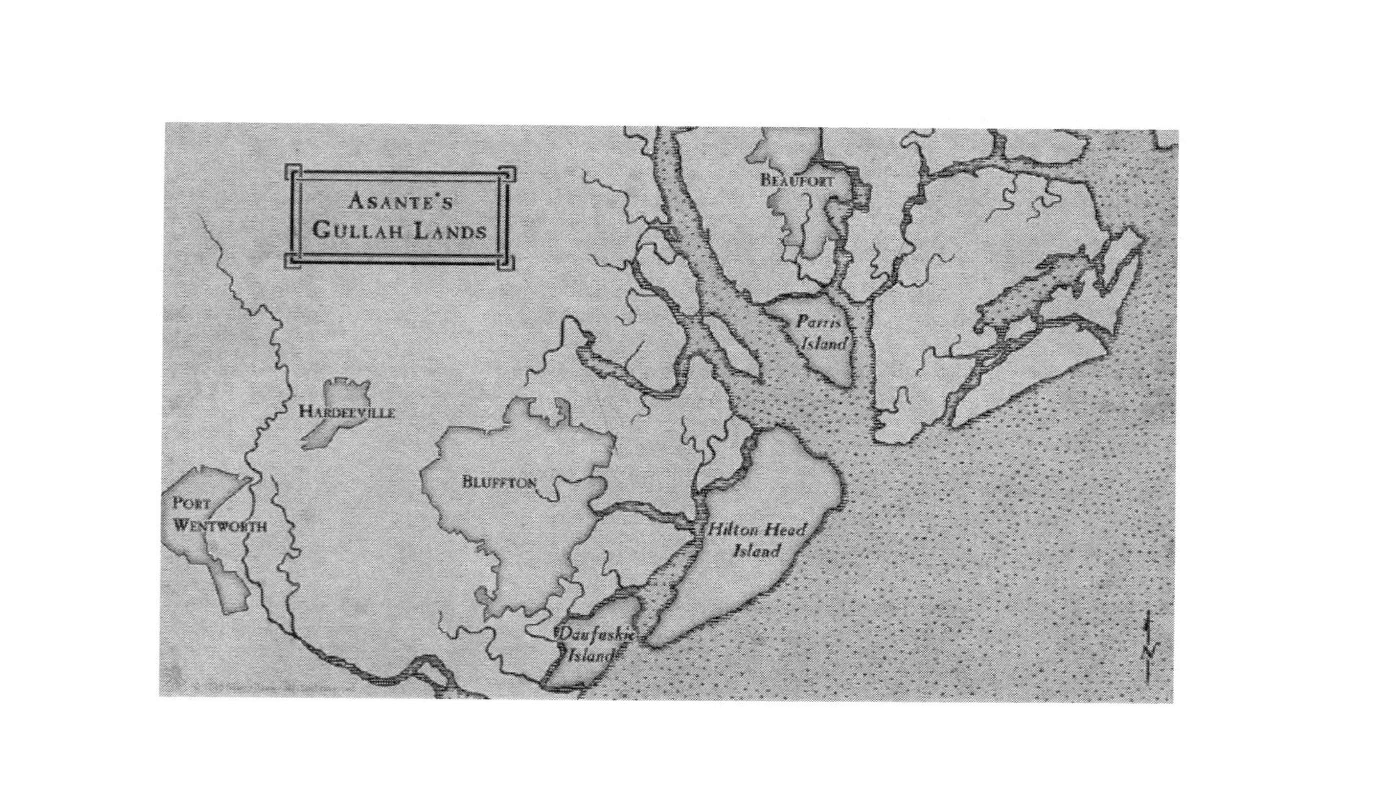
Asante's
Gullah Lands
Beaufort
Parris Island
Hardeeville
Bluffton
Port Wentworth
Hilton Head Island
Daufuskie Island
N

1 Farm - Warrior

Through remembering Beneda keeps the family farm alive.

A da geda weh A ain scatta seed

M'Deah often said that, *they harvested, without planting*. From her old Gullah Bible's book of Matthew. She explained it to mean, *work hard, even you think the bossman be lazy*. That way you ain't losing. No matter what happen, you done the best you can. M'Deah say, this apply to work 'round the farm. Planning for the future. Supporting the family. *Beneda, anything you should be doin, worth doin.* She say, *The family remember this. Always be loyal to this lesson, Beneda. Keep it close t' the heart.*

Beneda's seventeen, almost a woman, and thinks daily on Grandma's lessons. Spent every one of her one hundred and five years quoting to the young. Every day, on the farm, as Beneda rises with her mother and the workers, she remembers. As she toils, she hears that voice, still. As Beneda ends the day, she remembers M'Deah. *Family and farm are everything*. She's learned what is important, and tells herself she must work hard. Through remembering and working Beneda keeps the past alive in her heart.

Counting off on her fingers, she notes the work to inspect. One, check the equipment. Two, check weeding. Three, check pests. Four, check water level. She smiles as she stops in front of Jolan, *boy's growin' like a weed*. M'Deah would be proud of Jolan. Only eleven, but already one of Beneda's best workers.

"Jolan!" She stops to say, "I see you hard at work."

His smile brightens her day. "Beneda!" His small hand holds up a short scythe blade. "The silks are browning."

"Yes. That's right." She's proud of his awareness, Beneda's adopted worker has a sharp eye for harvesting cycles. "Soon it be time to gather in the corn." Beneda reaches for his scythe. Immediately, he picks another to run the sharping stone along. Beneda admires each of his strokes on both blade sides.

A steady hand guiding the stone with a rolling motion over the blade. Beneda watches. "You good at that." His quick smile accepts her praise. "Best you take care your turned strokes curl toward the tip." Jolan, he nods in agreement.

She hands back the blade and promises, "I see if cook make something special for supper tonight."

"Thanks, Beneda!"

"'Course. I'ma check the weeders. Keep up you good work." If all her workers were like Jolan, Beneda's job would be easy.

Her eyes scan the crop. Row on row of corn on each side, near high as Jolan's shoulder. Hardly any smell of corn pollen left. Just a faintsweet, cloying scent. This year's harvest might be a good one, M'Deah would be proud. Wiping sweat from her forehead, Beneda thinks about everything that can still go wrong.

If it gets hotter, or too much rain. Or not enough.

The weeders should be working the south acre.

Heading that way, she examines the stalks she passes. Glancing down row by row, admiring the straightness and the bright green stalks going to dun. Her feet stop suddenly. In the distance, a disturbing sight. Feet, not moving. Maybe, one hundred meters ahead. Sticking into her row.

She quickly unslings her bow, pulling an arrow from her quiver. Starting to run, *What could've happened? The weeders, attacked by a wolf? A bear?*

Running to the end of the row, she wonders, *Where everybody?* A quick frantic inventory in her mind. Mama in the big house. Jolan back near the steps. *He has blades.* Old Willy, he be at the stables. Nat and Angel on pest control, on the north acreage. Tyrone and Sarah weeding. *Those feet be one a them?*

As she gets close to them feet, Beneda slows. Nocking her arrow, her head bobs in all directions. Eyes flash. *Danger?* Jumping past these feet she looks. It is Tyrone she sees. *Sarah be down too!*

Her arrow tip quivers in each direction. Seeing nothing, she kneels beside Tyrone. He moves. Looking closely shows Sarah's breathing, and she utters a hurting moan. Tyrone with the whites showing around his eyes, and bruises forming under his brow, circling to near his ear, tries speaking.

"Two men." Tyrone voices a raspy and rough explanation. "Warned us." Beneda looks around again. Wanting to hit something. Wanting revenge for these two in her perfect row.

"Why?" She wants to know what she needs to do. *Now*. M'Deah would know what all to do.

"They order us t' leave." He tries moving. Grunts with the pain. Stops. Sarah's been still all this time. But breathing, Beneda sees. Tyrone struggles to move his head, more to report. “Told us, new owners soon own this land. Said next time it be worse.”

Beneda is ready to kill something. “Damn.” So it’s about land. “Which way?”

Tyrone wheezes, “East.” Takes in a deep shuddery breath. “T’ward th’ creek.” As Beneda stands, he tries holding onto her arm, “They got clubs.”

“Take care of Sarah.” Moving away, Beneda unnocks the bow, calling back, “Find Jolan. Get to the house.”

There’s a shortcut to the creek. She knows this farm better than anyone. *Whatever has to be done. I’m ready.*

A boat. Empty still. Stopping, glancing out in both directions, up and down the bank, Beneda renocks and prepares for attack. Needs answers. If people are coming on the Washington place, she must stop them. Her farm, her family’s farm.

A few more steps and she freezes. *I knew it!*

Two men climb a fence to get to the boat. Beneda waits, stock still. *What to do?* Her bow can finish them even at this distance. Her eye’s that good. Her hand that steady. She mustn’t let them get too close. Big rough looking men. They black as coal. Leather head to foot. Probably trappers, *when they ain’t beating unarmed farm crew.*

The lead one spots her. “Hey!” Running a hand over his short red hair, he grabs a club at his belt. The other stops, his bald head gleaming in the sun.

Beneda wonders, *Maybe wasn’t such a good idea.*

Just over three meters away, she figures, maybe a bit less. Look even more dangerous than she imagined. Aiming for the redhead's trunk, she steels herself to fire at his heart, first move he make at her. A few seconds to nock and fire at the bald one after that. She wishes Old Willy were with her. Or someone.

"Stop." Her voice sounding far from daunting, more quavery than she'd planned. She imagines what they think. A teenage girl, alone, coming out of the woods. With just a bow, and a hundred-year-old one at that. "Who sent you." she demands.

"Run along back home, girl." Redhead. Don't look the least bit scared by no bow. *Okay,* Beneda decides, *let them go.*

She relaxes a fraction. Bow still up, but already planning to avoid this brawl. "What you told the ones you beat?"

Red slides his eyes to Baldy. With his scary smile he looks back to her. Shouts across the rocks of the shore, "You all should leave. You tell the man runs this place, girl. Leave. Thar's all."

Still not helpful. They look like thugs, not leaders. "Why?" The bow's still up. Still pointing. *I really need to know who sent 'em.* Beneda needs to take something back to Mama.

"The Washington family don't own this land no more." Stunned, she doesn't know what to say to that. "We come back, people *will* get hurt, hear?"

They casually trot the last few meters over to the boat and shove off, laughing. Beneda lowers her bow. And fades back into the wood

~~~
~~~

Mama's hands shake as she pours. "We in trouble, Beneda." Tea spills into cups for her daughter and Old Willy, the sassafras smelling like root beer. Beneda tries remembering the last time she's witnessed her mother, nervous like this. *Never*.

"How are they?" Beneda looks to Willy. The injured couple made it as far as Willy's shack. Jolan had to help Sarah the last of the way.

"Seem okay, Shelia." Willy frowns. Sharing the women's worry while he shares their tea. "Both doin' better, now." His deeply lined face twists into a black smile. "Sarah not suffer much. Good she faint so quickly."

Mama wrings her hands. She hasn't sat. Just stands at the stove and wrings those hands. "They stop hitting her when she fainted?"

Mama. She would keep looking for something hopeful in this mess.

"No." Old Willy shakes his head. "They kept up the beating. Said, they was *followin' orders*."

Beneda turns in anger, an elbow knocks the cup into her lap. "*Dog!*"

Mama orders, "No blaspheming in this kitchen." But Willy just reaches for a rag.

"This because someone wanted t' buy us out?" She wonders if she should blame Mama—for them's injuries.

Mama's head hangs a little. "You know men came two months ago, 'Neda. Them wanting to buy." Beneda nods. "Well…" She hesitates, slows, "Well, I didn't tell you. They came back. Them *agents*. They said we Washingtons don't own the land."

Beneda hears Redhead's words in her mind again.

Old Willy's tea cup slams down. "What they mean you don't?"

Mama's hands smooth her apron. "They claimed they got a document. Proves all these Gullah farms be owned by someone in Africa." That makes no sense to Beneda. *Africa?*

"Well, how they think they can take our land because of something in Africa?" Willy's fist is still on Mama's tablecloth.

Africa? Beneda'd never heard anything so crazy.

Mama gives them both a weary nod, finally stepping from the safety of the stove. "I weren't worried. But, they say a clipper ship be on it way from Liberia. To the Library. Here in the Carolinas, agents say. They say documents be comin' on it, t' prove new ownership."

Beneda thinks of M'Deah's stories. "What should we do?" Of the Washington line living on this land since afore the Civil War. She turns to Old Willy, first, then her mama.

For a second Mama looks fierce. "Well my mama and hers fought to hold this farm during the Collapse an' no way we gon' give up now."

"The librarians." Old Willy becomes thoughtful, takes a sip, and tells them, "They have land deeds." He looks between his bosses, mother and daughter. "You can get a copy. Prove Washingtons own this here farm."

Mama collapses into her stuffed reading chair. Pulling at the doily on the armrest, balling it up. After thinking a moment. She reaches for a quill pen and the ink bottle off the bookshelf, drags a box of writing papers from the little shelf Dadda built her near on twenty year ago. "Beneda." Mama scribbles, "I sendin' this letter with you to the librarians. Get a copy of our property deed."

"Yes. Mama." Thinking immediately about the forty kilometers, and of what she needs to take with her. "What about the farm? If them agents come back?"

Old Willy glances at Mama. "I give everybody a blade or stick." He taps the table with a callused finger. "Dey defend theyselves."

In her writing Mama pauses. "Give everyone the chance to leave. If they want." After a moment. "I will give them a month's pay. Thems that choose to leave." Willy nods, like he'd thought of it his self.

Beneda hates hearing this. Everyone has to stay. Stay an' be loyal. To her family. *Don't they?*

Old Willy's running his thoughts out loud now his tea's gone. "Jolan will have to stay." *He practically family*. "He got no one. With he mama dead, and his papa, no one knows where."

Beneda nods sadly. "I'll take him with me." Her thoughts range now, planning the trip. List come to her, *Feed for the horses, two, if Jolan comes, two days horse ride…*

2 African Clipper - Heart

Running across the street, dodging dogs and buckboards. She hopes she's in time, Stick could do so much damage. *He quick like that.* Lakisha looks around for help; the Bossman's threats echo in her ears, *Peanut! You lookin' for a flaying this early?* The littlest of the Stick's gang. Around her, the street bustles with early morning walkers and riders. No one looks like they'd do.

Two young women tote packages, but she can't stop them. *Only get a earful for bein' in th' way.* An older man and woman walk a dog, *no*. They wouldn't be any help, *gloves might get dusty*. Glancing down the long street to the dock Lakisha notices the tall masts of a clipper ship. *Mens!*

Another dog across the street, an African village dog, Lakisha recognizes from pictures in school. Her grandmam, Aleetha had set her off to sleep with stories of them villages. This here dog's got himself a big man in a vest. *A Librarian?*

The librarian studies Lakisha as she approaches. A hand out to sniff at. A smile for the man. Now his dog on its haunches watches her, and his master. *Please see the help I need, not just little me, barefoot.*

"Librarian? Help." It all comes tumbling out, "Stick's going to kill Peanut." His green eyes look blankly down at her. *Does he understand?* "Stick's beating Peanut. He'll kill him!"

"Peanut?" Is all the man asks. A big black hand rests on his dog's head

"A boy!" Lakisha pants out, leaving so many other words behind in her rush. "Hurry." Without waiting any longer, she turns and dashes back to the alley. *Footsteps.* He's following. Her spirits soar.

Getting close to Peanut's screams and the noise of the blows she's left to go find help, Lakisha halts. And upon her appearance, Stick takes a rest from Peanut's beating. The small boy lies curled on the ground. Stick's switch grows still.

Behind Lakisha, the Librarian steps up. Sets a hand on her slight shoulder. She can feel his dog's breaths on her wrist. Stick's eyes grow wide as he takes in this big black shape.

"Librarian?" He looks to this man's vest. Then to his dog. Then to his own bodyguard. "Here ain't no library business. Get lost." Lakisha, even at thirteen, knows now that Stick be needing reassurance of some back up.

The librarian moves a little forward. Making it clear he's going nowhere. "Sure. This isn't my concern. But what about the Peanut?"

Stick frowns, spitting at the ground. At the boy. "He works for me. I got a right to punish him."

Lakisha's big helper waits.

"I quit," comes from Peanut, weakly.

He shivers, but says it all the same. Even so near Stick's big boot. The Bossman stares now, only at Lakisha and the man with the vest.

A slow smile coming over his face, the librarian's eyes bore into Stick. "Seems he's no longer your employee. Can't punish him now."

Stick looks to his bodyguard. That man motions toward the librarian. *Make Stick think about what that vest means.*

"Okay. You can employ the boy. He eats a lot." He waves roughly down the alley, "Good luck. Let's go." The bodyguard and other small boys turn and follow. Like it's been Stick's idea all along, the cedar switch making its last whipping noise through the air.

~~~

With her arm around Peanut, Lakisha feels a shiver of embarrassment run through her, for bringing a librarian to her mother's home. They arrive at the tenement where chickens run and peck around the dusty lanes. "Mama stays here." Being brave, she points the librarian to the door, third in a row of seven. "She share with friends she work with." Peanut is leaning on her arm a bit less. Feeling better now.

The scout, *Asante*, he's told the pair, bows his head, a hand to his vest. "You honor me."

Peanut whispers soft in Lakisha's ear, "He talk like the mayor."

"Come on." She tugs at the little one. "You come an' stay with Mama for a while." Looking at the sun, Lakisha figures, *Yes, she be home*. "Mama!"

Mama comes in from the kitchen, slow on her feet and wiping flour on her apron. "Lord, girl, what you got here?" She takes a moment looking over the tall man in his vest. "Ain't never had a librarian in my house."

"Auntie." He gives what Lakisha is thinking of as
~~~

his traditional bow. "Thank you for welcoming me."

Turning back to her daughter, Mama points at Peanut. "What dis?"

Lakisha pulls the little one close, his head barely up to her chest. "Dis be Peanut." *Mebbe the librarian's nice bow make Mama feel kindly.*

"What a Peanut?" Lakisha knows what that means.

"Peanut. He left Stick." Mama frowns at that name. "Him need a place to bide." In the silence, she examines Mama's face. *Seems better, not angry*. "He don't eat much. Will you Peanut?" Peanut, he nods his head like he been offered some.

Mama's lips hint at a smile. "Lil' boys *always* eat a lot." Looking over the runt. "How old de Peanut?"

"I'm six!" he brags; loudest thing Lakisha's ever hear from him.

Mama lets out an exasperated sigh. "Okay. Peanut. You stay, awhile." A finger taps at his head, "Gots to cleanup, though. First thing."

"Thank you, Mama. We set up a pallet near me, right, Peanut?"

Turning her eyes back to the big man, Mama gives him the similar top to bottom she gave Peanut. Mama's head cocks. "How we help de library?"

"Asante." His fingers rest on his chest again. "I travel to the library at Bluffton, South Carolina."

"Dat accent." Mama looks at him some more. "You a salt-water African?"

"Yes Ma'am. I have arrived on a ship just this day." He touches his vest and the hilt of the sword at his waist. "I am a library scout from Kenya." The scout waves behind him, to his dog waiting at Mama's door. "Myself and Aza."

Mama is beaming now. “My, my. A librarian *an’* a African. In my home on the same day.”

Lakisha wonders, *How can I help this librarian?* “Bluffton! That be ’bout a day walk.” Her grandmam schooled her early, on maps and such. “You know the way?”

He taps the bag at his side. “My instructions say arrive at Port Wentworth and *travel* to Bluffton.” He smiles at her offer. “Any help you can offer would be appreciated, I confess, I don’t know the way.”

Lakisha gives a pleading look to Mama. Who considers a moment. “Okay, Lakisha can guide you. She grown enough for that task.” Mama glances at Peanut, then back to the scout. “Make sure, she don’t walk home by herself.” She reaches into a cup on a bare shelf, and draws out a few coins.

With a stern look to Peanut, Mama scolds, “You even think bout lookin’ in that cup and I’ll hand you over to Stick m’ownself.” Then that black glance moves back to her daughter. “You bring me a child to care for, then leave on a trip. Who gonna clean him up?”

“Come on Peanut.” Lakisha grabs his hand, pushing to the washbasin out back. “Quick, before Mama change her mind.”

“Scout Asante,” Lakisha hears as she walks out. “I feel bad spending hardly no time with my lil’ girl…” Over the pump’s gush of water, she hears no more.

~~~

“Just down this road.” Lakisha points ahead. “We get the boat across to the mainland. Once we get there it be mostly dry, don’t need nothing; but our feets.”
~~~

The old clock on Mama's wall had said near seven when they left, a good hour or more of sun. "It be under a kilometer. Fer sure." They should reach the boat in time.

"How far is it to Bluffton?"

She glances up at the sun and thinks of the path to Bluffton in her mind's eye. "Thirty kilometers, ifn' we make that boat."

"That's a long way in a day."

"We might can catch a ride. Part way, find a bateau."

Asante's pace has picked up a bit. He talks as they move, "Your Mama had some fine knives hanging."

Lakisha takes longer steps and answers, "She work in the cannery." Her voice shows pride in Mama's hard work.

Asante puts on a big smile. "Where's your Papa?" Lakisha wants to be proud of Papa too.

"He can fix machines. He had to go off for work. He send money to Mama. When he can."

"Good."

"He been gone for years. Now." Lakisha only remembers his smell. His work hardened hands. How he made Mama smile.

The scout gives a grave nod. "Why don't you have to be in school?"

She thinks of her best friend, Veronika, working in her folk's orchards this week. "We got two months off for harvest." The pair walk, silent for a bit, and Lakisha falls to thinking about whether she should work at her mother's job this summer.

"How often do you travel this road?" The scout examines the wide dirt path, and dense bushes on each side.

“Couple times a year.” Lakisha thinks about last time, in the rain, and mud. “When her bosses give her extra cans, we travel to the big town to get better prices. Selling them.”

“What your Mama mean, salt-water African?” He cocks his head at her. Lakisha smiles. Amused she knows more than a librarian.

“Round here, black folks call theyselves, Lowcountry Africans.” She thinks of the many insulting Gullah and Geechee names that get thrown around. “People born in Africa be salt-water Africans. Cus they have t’ come cross the salt water. Have *to* come *across*.”

He laughs. In the lowering sun, Lakisha admires the beadwork on his vest. “I hear Africa’s huge.” She imagines herself taking the long voyage there. “How much have you seen?”

The big black man laughs again. “Yes. It is so big; I’ve only reached some parts. Though I’ve traveled from east to west. Seen the Indian Ocean. The Cape of Good Hope, in the south. Dipped my feet in the Mediterranean. But, I’ve not seen it all.”

“*Dog!!*” Lakisha’s face burns, at her cussing that way, but she’s just amazed and fascinated. *I need become a librarian.* “You must travel all the time.”

She’s surprised at his quick look of pain. Until it turns to a faint smile. “I feel I always travel. I’ve only spent a few days at my home, in Bungoma, in the last two years.”

Lakisha sees an old man approach, with a goat cart. She don’t know him, but gives a friendly wave. The old man smiles, then notices the library scout, giving him a respectful bow.

After he passes by, Asante's expression becomes serious. "How do you know Peanut?"

She thinks about the trouble those boys cause. "Stick be small time. A gangster. He runs a group of kids in town. They pickpocket, steal fruit. Anything they get they hands on."

"Don't you have a sheriff?"

"Sheriff, he get money from Stick." Lakisha remembers the last election day, the big fat sheriff givin' speeches and getting elected year after year. "That's what people say." She thinks about her first run-in with Peanut. "Peanut try pickin' my pocket. He weren't but a nubbin." She laughs. "Maybe five years old."

The scout's mouth quirts in a half frown. "So young?"

"Yep. Stick claims he be carin' for them lil orphans. Provide a roof over they heads. Food every day." She shakes her head. *People do anything to survive.* "Well, after stopping Peanut, 'bout a year ago, we get t' be friends."

Asante looks down at her, taking this all in. "What do kids do for careers in Port Wentworth?"

Careers? She thinks about Mama. In the cannery. About Peanut, then her own future. "Not much. 'Specially orphans.' I might work with Mama in the cannery."

"What do you want to do?" He pauses, the sun's nearly gone now. "What are your dreams?"

"Don't know." She thinks about how to avoid the cannery. The knives. The fish smells. Impossible to remove from Mama's clothes. "I like the Lowcountry. I don't hope to leave. But, I want to help folk. Want to be needed."

3 Trees – Soul

Jolan's feet hurt. He glances with envy at Beneda's sandals. *Wish I had some good uns'. Her pants ain't cutoffs neither.*

"Beneda. Why ain't we take the horses?"

"Too much cost to take the ferry," she answers, "'sides, harvest soon. Workers need them horses."

Jolan tries not to whine, but hears himself, "When we get a rest?"

She gives him a fierce gander. "Don't you complain. We ain't barely left, not even been walking more'n half a hour."

"Ah. Ain't we been walking for hours?" *If'n I had shoes, I'd shut up.* Pretty sure his grumble had been heard if not listened to.

"It been maybe twenty minutes." She glances up to the sun. Then points ahead. "We'll be near the Harris place soon."

Jolan hopes they stop there and get sumin' to eat. He takes out the knife Beneda let him bring. Its blade shines in the sunlight.

"Don't go playin' with that," she scolds. "It be for cutting fruit, not play." He frowns, grumpy, but slips it back in its sheath.

Following her there on the dirt track road, he thinks, *ain't no fruit on this road anyways*. But he keeps that thought to hisself.

Climbing Aster and Goldenrod blooms on each side of the path. J*us like 'round the Washington place. Nothin' new. Jus a bunch of walkin', walkin', walkin'.* Jolan plods behind Beneda. His step not as long. She be tall, for a girl. He's mesmerized watching Beneda's bow hung on her back. His head droops down, and now his eyes follow the hem of her pants, above those sandaled feet.

She stops suddenly. Jolan reckons, *she holding a breath.* He gazes in surprise; she's unslung her bow. Pulls an arrow and nocks it. His eyes follow the tip's direction. There stands a huge black shape next to a cypress. *Bear!* It looks at them and lets lose a *huufff.*

Frozen, Jolan stops. Looks at Beneda with fear. She's released her arrow and reaches for another. Back at the bear, the arrow's stuck in the tree's trunk, inches from the black bear's head.

It smells the arrow, then gives a second loud *huff* as it turns, lumbering heavy-footed, and retreats slowly into the woods.

Jolan glances between the tree and Beneda, then back to the bear as it shuffles away. "*Dang!*" She puts her second arrow back up in her quiver, and the bow back on her shoulder.

Beneda check on him. Smiles. "Please get my arrow." Jolan nods and trots over. "Be careful."

Jolan gets to it, keeping a lookout for the bear.

He tugs at the tree where it's caught. The arrow won't budge. Deep in the cypress. "It stuck." Grunting, he keeps at it. Finally, Beneda walks up, as he gets it to come loose. "That was hard."

Beneda, taking the arrow, squats down, pulls a rag out of her bag and wipes its tip. "It be a very strong bow."

Jolan thinks, in case a bear comes back, and asks, "How I get a strong bow?"

She pulls at his shoulder to get back on the path. "You need a grandma who leaves you hers." She grins, then pulls it off and hands it to him.

As Jolan turns it over, his hand follows the sharp curve at each end. "From you grandma?"

"Yes." Beneda takes the bow back. "This be a composite bow. Made more than one hundred years ago."

Jolan don't know anyone that old. "She use it?"

Beneda gives a funny glance. "M'Deah used it against folks wanting to take her land."

"Can you teach me? To use this here bow?" He begs, "'case there be bears where we goin'."

"We'll see." Beneda walks faster. He hurries to keep up. *That good as a yes.*

The path stretches on endlessly. Jolan sees no one on the road. *But, someone use it. This path be clear an' smooth.*

Jolan works on moving his legs, his feet feel sore. A steady lifting of each foot, behind Beneda's. His eyes track back and forth from her to the trail ahead. *Will more bears come?*

"How much farther must we go?" Jolan groans, slows down. "We're never gon' get there!"

~~~

At last Beneda points up the road. "We near the Harris place. Jus'a bit now."

Jolan looks hard at the fence out front of the Harris entrance. "Don't I see someone der?"

Beneda focuses on the Harris's wood and wire
~~~

gate. "Yes. I think it be lil' Caleb. Go find what he want." Jolan sprints on his toes. *Sure 'nough. It be him. He folks work for Old Lady Harris.* Caleb's younger, only nine.

"Hey Caleb!" A smile as he runs. "Whatcha' doin' since school?"

"Jolan!" Caleb looks the older boy up n' down. "That a nice knife you got!" Stopping before pulling it out. Jolan slaps the hilt in pride.

Minding Beneda's scolding about it. *Cutting fruit, not play*. Jolan asks, "Whatcha doin' out here?" remembering why Beneda sent him running ahead.

Caleb glances back up the long country road. *He 'member too.* "Lady Harris want you wait."

"Why for?" *Guess the old lady watched them come up from her top window or out on the widow's walk she got up there on the roof.* "Why we s'pose to wait?"

"Lady want t' know. Beneda going to Bluffton?"

Jolan nods. "We headed der now."

Caleb sets to nodding too. "Lady wants you wait. She's a comin' along too." With that, Caleb turns and takes off toward the big house. before Beneda even comes up.

"What he want?" Beneda stops behind him, asking.

Jolan points to the almost invisible Caleb nearing the big house now. "He say Lady Harris say to bide."

"What?" She stares at the house.

"Caleb say, Lady Harris comin' wit us." He notices, and points, "Dey coming! Out the house. Hope Caleb come wif' us." *I show him my knife, tell 'im, it for fruit, not playing.*

Beneda sets down her pack. "We'll see." And the

pair wait for them others.

Jolan spies the powder-white hair coming up. A small bag hangs at her side. Missus Harris' shoulder covered in a white knit shawl. Her grandboy beside her. *That be Pete,* Jolan remembers, *Been in school wif Beneda.*

"Well, Beneda Washington." A bossy air surrounds the old lady. "You a'headed t' Bluffton?" She frowns before even hearing Beneda's reply.

"Yas'um, Miss Harris."

"I reckon you can call me Old Lady, like all the young'ns." She pulls Pete close beside her. "We make the journey with you." Beneda nods. "You about these thieves try'n to take our farms? You know my grandson, Pete."

Beneda approaches Lady Harris to take her hands. "Yas'um, Mama sent me to get a copy our property papers." She drops the Lady's hands. Gives a wave to Pete.

The old woman shoves Pete over, then waves back toward the house. "Caleb asks to come too. I tell him he can." Jolan spies Caleb on the pathway running full tilt, a pack over his shoulder.

Beneda smiles at Caleb's crazy run. "You hear from the other farms, Lady Harris?"

"Oh yeah, chile, lotsa them be sending folks to check the records." She grabs at Caleb and checks him over. *Him barefoot too.* "I'ma meet some in Bluffton. You should meet 'em too."

Beneda picks up the pack she's set down, ready to get going again. "Okay."

Lady looks at Beneda, up and down, up and down. "Lordy, girl. You g'tting' to be grown! You got your grandma's bow?"

“Yas’um.” Beneda runs a hand along the bow at her shoulder.

Lady’s hand on her grey hair, shoving wisps back under her bonnet. “I remember your grandma firing across a field. Arrow after arrow. The crop a burning. Shouts of fight’n so loud. The lord above must’ve have heard.”

Pete’s eyes roll in he head. “Gra’ma…”

“Let’s all move on.” Lady Harris up and movin’ to swing the gate now. “Sooner we make the crossin’ the sooner we be done.”

~~~

Approaching the crossing, Jolan’s ears fill with the sound of rushing water. Looking over his shoulder, he’s first. No one waits yet. He’s noticed Pete try to talk to Beneda. But Beneda, she moves over to Caleb and takes his hand. Old Lady walks ahead, not even noticing. *She got some strong legs that one.* Across the water, Jolan spies the boatman, dropping passengers on the far shore. Soon their group all waits on the shore

“Won’t be long now.” Beneda waves, and Caleb and Jolan follow her lead. She tall, might be the only hand the ferryman see from afar. “He be back to take us soon.”

“I’m scared o’ boats.” Caleb shakes like a wet dog, Jolan feels a bit sorry for him.

“Ah, honey. Ain’t nothing to fear.” Old Lady grabs at him, squashing the boy to her apron then swats his backside. “We all come here by boat.”

Pete, he shakes his head, groans, “Don’t tell about Igbo Landing, gra’ma!”

Lady scowls at her grandson. “Why not? All
~~~

folks need t' hear that one." Jolan hopes that face she aims, that glower, stays on her grandson, not him. He like stories. But then she peer at Beneda. "Girl, you know de story?"

"Yes, Lady." Beneda nods, a good girl, she gives the old one her smile. "I heard."

Lady casts her eyes on the boys. "You young'ns hear the story?" Both Jolan and Caleb's heads shake. "Well, now's soon enough."

She spies some shade under a big cypress. Shuffles over the meter or two, waving everyone to come join her. "Sit you down, Pete, get comfortable. I'ma tell 'em the story of Igbo Landing."

Jolan settles in the shade, aside Caleb. Pete steps close to Beneda and Old Lady leans back against the tree.

Lady takes a deep breath, adjusting her shawl, in the distance a shout can be heard from the far bank. "In the last century of slavery in this land. Long ago, now, back so many generations you need more'n two hands to count.

"Black people from Igbo in Africa got seized and put on a ship to America, in chains." She wipes her brow. Bringin' out a water flask, she drinks deep.

"About three score folks, they say. All ages, down to lil' ones." Jolan has heard similar stories. The old days, when black folks labored on the farms. Slaves.

"Then the whole lot of these Igbo was sold to a master on St. Simon Island. They all delivered by small boat. From Savannah." She stops, glancing to each of them. Then she stares across the rushing water. *Is she looking at boats returning?*

"Then they git unloaded from the boat ont' the

swampy land, in chains. The Igbo leader looks at his people. He looks at his new master. He spy the deep water, of the swamp. He gives a command. The people they all fin' to sing a hymn of they land. And, they march together into the water. The master and he men try to stop it. Many Igbo get they freedom that day."

"Bu-but, did they die?" Caleb wants to know. "The Igbo?"

Old Lady Harris frown, then smiles at Caleb. "Yes, many died, but they not slaves."

Pete waves everyone up. "The boat! Ya'll hurry, let's cross."

4 Big House - Trickster

The raggedy man shakes like a leaf. He afraid. “I don’ know, Cootuh…” They be waiting at the guard gate, a’front of the big house.

“Don’t worry youself, Jeremiah.” Cootuh’s one hand grabs his wrist, holds him in the wagon. “You goin’ be alright.”

Holding the reins of two fine horses drawing the empty wagon, Cootuh tries distracting the nervous man for the few minutes it takes to step up to the mansion. That there Nehemiah, he runs up in his livery, in perfect order, inspects the wagon with a vigilant eye before waving forward.

“Mister Buckra expecting us.” Cootuh includes Jeremiah, with a sure nod, as they pass Nehemiah. Stopping near the steps, Cootuh jumps down. Jeremiah follows, on unsteady steps, up to the big oak door. Faith, in her maid outfit, stands waiting to do her curtsy, she waves Cootuh and the fearful one in with a soft smile.

Cootuh pushes Jeremiah, who’s stopped to take in the grand chandelier, in wonder. It hangs down with fifty lit candles throwing their light into the room. Mister Buckra’s main staircase extends up, with wide carpeted steps on each riser. Looking up, Cootuh gazes longingly as Octavia descends.

Octavia's skin seems to glow. Bronze highlighted by long jet black hair. Her steps in that long white dress show her feeling of royalty. Cootuh knows she's aware of the effect she has. On men. He bows his head.

"Welcome home, Mister Cootuh." Her eyes glaze past the raggedy one beside him. She nods curtly in Jeremiah's direction.

"Is your father at home, Miss?" Cootuh sees Jeremiah tries not staring at his shift of manner. Cootuh tries not staring at that perfect face.

"Yes, he has returned," her words are for her own show, no eyes meet as she pronounces this. Octavia turns and ascends without waiting, or a look back. "Come this way," the two are invited.

Jeremiah stumbles on the carpet. The wood paneling absorbs the flickering light while the many mirrors bounce twinkling slivers around them. Cootuh grabs his arm to steady him, squeezing.

Octavia precedes them into the big room to the left. It's like she forgets them. Cootuh sticks his head in. Mister Buckra sits in a comfortable chair, set perfectly at an angle for gazing out the windows. Cootuh always admires that view of the river and Mister Buckra's green fields.

Malcolm, his lieutenant, gives Cootuh his usual pained expression. Then, seeing Jeremiah, that look really turns sour. "Cootuh." The name drips disdain. "What have you brought us?"

Cootuh reaches back, pulling Jeremiah up beside him. "Suh, Mister Buckra, Jeremiah here works one of the farms we interested in." Jeremiah, next to him, shaking like a leaf, offers a weak smile.

"Excellent. Malcolm, get our guest something to

drink." Eying his daughter. "Honey, you want something?"

Octavia glances back from staring out the window. "Just a seltzer." Her father waves to Malcolm.

Malcolm frowns as he walks over to the liquor cart. He turns to face Jeremiah. "What you want?"

"I…I drink r—rum."Jeremiah quakes, a deer in a bright light, shrugs.

Malcolm nods, not asking Cootuh, probably feels it's beneath him to. He starts pouring. "I'll take seltzer, too." Malcolm casts an evil look Cootuh's way, before pulling out a second glass. Then he holds both glasses out. Waits.

Cootuh smiles, moving over to take them. Mister Buckra weighs the exchange as Cootuh bows to Octavia and holds a glass out, with a little smirk. Turning, he faces Malcolm, another glass out toward him. He moves back and takes it to Jeremiah.

Mister Buckra waits for Jeremiah to swallow his sip. "You work on one of the Gullah farms?"

Jeremiah coughs, then raises his head from his glass. "Yas'um, Mister Buckra." The drink sloshes in his hand as he waves to the east. "I work on Old Lady Harris's place."

Cootuh tries to steady him with a hand on Jeremiah's shoulder, stepping in to explain, "Jeremiah here, is interested in changing employment."

The headman smiles down into his trimmed beard. "Is that true?"

Cootuh feels it, Jeremiah continuing to shake. "Yas'um. I hear th' Harris family won't own th' place fa' long." He looks at his drink as it moves in his glass. He doesn't raise it. He recites, just like

Cootuh's schooled him to, "I want t' work for someone who will—own it."

Buckra gives a nod, he smiles at his daughter, then back to Malcolm. He pronounces, succinctly, "That is a wise decision." Turning. "Cootuh. Settle our new man in the bunkhouse. We will need more employees once the property has changed hands."

Silently, Malcolm demands the glass back.

~~~

Back up the wide carpeted stairs, as Cootuh approaches, he hears Malcolm speaking to the big boss. Stands at the door, not entering for a moment.

Malcolm continues something, "…they have not all. We have sent the men two times, but—"

Buckra interrupts, "I don't care what you have to do. The investors are getting impatient."

Cootuh knocks now, a heavy hand to say, *Ooops. I am back*. He pushes on the door and it opens further, so he enters.

Of course, Malcolm ignores him. Octavia gives Cootuh a stare as he walks in. *She suspects?* He stops in front of the window, where the boss stands, gazes out. Waits.

Mister Buckra runs his hand over his neat beard, he pauses before announcing, "This plan of ours will employ thousands." He points out the wide window. In the direction of the workers' barracks. "We're helping the people. Those farms have a handful of workers now. When we get those ten, we will change the economy."

Malcolm turns away and rolls his eyes. Cootuh can read what he thinks of noble speeches.

"Father. You said we would have the land in time
~~~

for this planting season." Octavia brings the talk back to the point.

"Malcolm, step it up." The Big Boss waves to Cootuh. "Take him. Just don't let anything lead back to me."

With a cruel grin crossing before his eyes, Malcolm nods, and the boss continues, jabbing at the air with his cigar, "We'll need to find what will make them leave. Go undercover among them. Find the farmers. Find a weakness. Who their leaders are. What will break them."

With that he stalks out the room. The three remaining face each other. Cootuh with a question. Octavia looking bored, Malcolm's eyes glint with scheming.

Cootuh speaks first, "What do you need me to do? Boss."

Intent on the trees and grounds for a moment, Malcolm surveys the grounds out the window. "We need to know why these farmers are holding on. They're just poor Gullah families." He seems lost in thought. "Why don't they take our money and leave?"

"Their blood is in the land." Octavia takes a last sip from her glass. Setting it down she walks out the door. Cootuh grins at Malcolm's confusion. *Good.*

Turning back to Cootuh. "What's she mean?"

Cootuh puts on a crooked smile. *Now he talks to me.* "Miss Octavia, she mean they have buried their parents and grandparents on those farm."

A small look of realization comes stealing onto Malcolm's face. Cootuh states what should be so obvious, "The land means more than money."

~~~
~~~

Find the farmers. Cootuh thinks about his mission in this bar, eighteen hours later, in Bluffton. He chose Bluffton, the largest town near the Gullah farms Mister Buckra needs. They get supplies in this town. Just like when he was young. He sips on his whiskey and talks to himself, silently in his head. His family would come to town to shop and sell. When Cootuh was living with his farmer parents. Another life. He found Jeremiah here.

Under Cootuh's elbow, the bartender wipes down the counter. "Another?" He points at the glass.

Cootuh shakes his head. "Where are the farmers?"

The bartender glances into the far corner. "You just missed them." Pointing into the dark across the room. "Was a table full an hour ago. Only one left."

Cootuh inventories this farmer's outfit. Worn overalls, but clean. A mended shirt. *Poor but proud*. He orders another drink after all. Walking over, he practices his, "I'd like to buy you a round. Figured whiskey would suit."

But the man turns a suspicious gaze on him when Cootuh delivers the line aloud. "Now, why would you?" he asks.

Cootuh sets the drink down. But, doesn't sit yet. "I want to ask your advice." When the other nods, then he sits. "I work for someone, over to Hardeeville, getting his self a farm in the Lowcountry. I want advice, about crops and planting schedules."

The farmer gives him one more hard look, eyes the drink being offered, then relaxes. "Okay."

Cootuh reaches his hand over the sticky table. "Cootuh. Like I said, Hardeeville."

"Turner. From the Brown farm." This Turner

shakes his hand.

Cootuh sits at the large round table, looking across to the farmer. “So, what you grow?”

“Corn, soybeans, and small vegetable plots.” Turner’s eyes take on a far off gaze. “I don’t know how much longer we’ll be workin’.”

Cootuh cocks his head, looks like he’s about to agree, *I know that*. Thinks, *he’s right.* So it’ll show on his face. “What you mean?”

The farmer shakes his head. Looking sad now. “Someone tryin’ to buy our farms. Won’t take *no* f’a answer.”

Cootuh swallows awkwardly. Makes a point of not keeping his eyes on his glass. Looks the man right in his. Before asking, “What’ca doin’ about it?”

His face turns fierce. “We never leave our land.”

5 Library Scout - Heart

Lakisha had been impressed by this building, but never before thought to enter. She follows the scout now, borrowing his bravery. Long shadows of trees dapple those white walls. Four large pillars stand waiting at the front, wider than she can stretch her thin arms across. Lakisha staggers. Relieved the day's hike is almost over. Rubbery legs wobble on the steps up to the library's oak doorway.

"Aza. Wait here." The scout leaves the dog sitting on the top step.

Inside Lakisha is ready to squat like the dog. Her bones weary. A woman stands up behind a desk in the marbled room. Her long flowing robes dark shades of maroon and purple.

"Scout?"

Setting his bag on the marble. "Yes." He bows. "Asante. From Africa. I am here for the Librarian."

Returning his bow, the receptionist indicates stone benches against the wall. "I will summon Librarian Oliver." Pointing to a high table. "There is cool water. In the stoneware jug, just there."

Only glancing after the flowing robes swirling out of the room, Lakisha plods over and pours into a cup. Drinking, she thinks of the scout's dog. "Should I take some to Aza?"

"Yes, thank you." The scout takes a silent stance. Reminds Lakisha of when soldiers came to Port Wentworth. Standing in rows. Stiff as statues. For hours, in the town square.

Coming back through the door, hands wet with water and dog slobber, Lakisha spies an old man approaching Asante. In the lights cascading from the high windows his vest sparkles as well. She stares, *them beads on his vest be polished!*

"Ah, scout." His hands reaches. "Welcome to the library at Bluffton. Come into my meeting room." His hand guides Lakisha's companion into another space, then Librarian Oliver says, "Thank you, Zenobia." But Lakisha, who trails behind, he ignores.

A smell fills the room, she notices it stepping into the room, coming from the stacks of books on the desks, shelves, floor. Rows of books on rows of books. Levels of them except near the windows. Ceiling-high shelving surrounds them, rows in a space easily five meters on each side with a couple of meters height above their heads. Lakisha neck stretches taking it in.

"You have some papers for me?"

Asante reaches into his pack. "Here are the results of the libraries' investigations."

"Ah. From Liberia." Taking the large stack of papers, the librarian comments, "That's a lot."

"Apparently, a man calling himself Geechee Freeman landed there, in 1883. Claimed to own one thousand acres of bottom land in the United States Lowcountry."

The librarian shakes his head slowly, a skeptical glance up at the scout. "That's quite a story."

"Seems he tried several times to sell his claimed

land. Nobody believed him, so whatever he possessed passed to his children."

Librarian Oliver waves Asante to a chair. Lakisha stands. "He had some?"

"Yes. We found someone who claims to be a descendant. Of course, we can't verify his identity."

Taking a seat, steepling his fingers, the older man inquires, "How valid is that original claim?"

Asante counters, "We have no reason to believe it. It's that dead man's word against your records."

Lakisha stays silent, but watches how Oliver's brows raise and his lower lip quivers. *Maybe he embarrassed.* He utters, "I was afraid you were going to say that."

"What's the problem?"

The Librarian's hands rub together, she sees his frown of discomfort as he admits, "The records have disappeared."

"Just those records?" Asante is frozen, staring at the other man.

"Yes." He pats the air, then slices it with his hand. "It is suspicious. Just the records for ten adjacent Gullah Lowland farms."

Asante's fingers stroke his lip. "How could that happen?" Lakisha, stock-still listens, quiet as a mouse in this big room of books.

"It should not be possible. The records are public," At this admission Librarian Oliver ducks his head. "Anyone can look at them. Though we do check bags when people leave after viewing records."

The scout looks at the papers he's handed this befuddled man. *Wantin' to grab them back?* He asks softly, "Could someone on staff have moved them?"

"I questioned everyone. Personally. But, the

problem is—I don't know *when* they disappeared."

"What can be done?" The scouts voice is calm.

Lakisha wonders, *This here trip all a waste?*

Librarian Oliver scratches, looks at Lakisha, like he's seeing her for the first time. She thinks, *He thinkin' I'm to blame?*

He goes on, fingers still in that steeple, "Fortunately there are backup files in Beaufort." His eyes examine the scout, something lights up and he asks, "Would you be willing to travel there?"

"Of course. How far?"

"Close, only a day's travel." Lakisha thinks of the two days it took her mama and her to make that walk. Thinks of the sun in their faces most all the way. "It's already dark. You must eat. We have a nice room for you."

"And Lakisha."

The Librarian frowns, viewing Lakisha's bare feet. Finally, he nods. "Yes. Your guide as well. The cleaning staff —no, I will have Zenobia get one ready for her." Then he turns away and heads to the door. "We ate an hour ago. Let's see if cook has anything for you."

That woman in the robe rises as they enter the lobby. "Zenobia. Can you see if Cook can get anything together for our scout— and his guest?"

Giving a bow to Asante, the Librarian takes a step back now, head nodding. "I'm so glad you are here to help us. I'll speak to you tomorrow."

Zenobia waves the pair toward another door.

~~~

At Zenobia's call, a portly woman hurries into the dining room, tucking a wash rag into her apron.
~~~

"Yas'um? Somethin' more for the Librarian?"

"No, dear. These guests have just arrived. What do we have for them? Anything for some sore bodies will do." At this Zenobia looks back to Asante. "Something warm. Yes?

"Anything. Thank you, Cook." He bows, and Lakisha, a quick learner, follows suit.

Scooting around the long table, Cook spies Lakisha rising from her bow. "Two a yuhs? Yas'um. I'll see they set for the night." Rubbing her hands on her apron, she beams at the pair. "Not much ready. But I get you somethin'."

Zenobia places a hand on Lakisha's arm, "Sit child." Before she leaves them to the Cook's dining room.

"Honey child, where you from?" the Cook asks.

"Port Wentworth. We walked. Missus." Bowing again. *Like Asante would.*

"That be a long way. You needs some good food. *Ummhum*. And you can call me Jennifer." The big woman hurries out, listing things aloud, *soup, gravy, biscuits…*

Asante sits, he studies his hands. Then he surveys Lakisha at his side. "Well, you can go back home tomorrow. After a good night's sleep. I appreciate your work, especially with Aza."

"I can go wit you to Beaufort."

A head shake. Hands steepled like the Librarian Oliver. "Your mama'll worry."

"I'll send her a letter. I can write."

"You can? You been to Beaufort?"

"Oh yes." She nods, hearing what the librarian said, *half ways to a yes*. "It took mama an' me two days to reach there."

Cook carries in a tray. Steam lifts up from a stewy broth in two bowls. Wonderful smells hit Lakisha's nose as Cook sets them out on the polished table. "Here be hearty vegetable soup." putting down two plates. "Sorry, nothin' mor'n gravy and bread."

Asante gives a big smile. "This is wonderful. We are grateful."

Lakisha coughs out, "Yeah." But she can't wait. Her spoon dips instantly into the thick soup. *Uum, good*. Beans, carrots, celery…

Cook Jennifer backs out smiling, eyes on the quiet scout and Lakisha. Only the sounds of slurping and clicks of utensils break the silence.

When the bowls and plates are almost cleaned, the Scout speaks again. "Make sure you write your mama. First thing in the morning."

Nodding, Lakisha sops up the last of the gravy. "You think libraries need writers, like me? Wonder if cook needs a worker, mebbe?" Grabbing the last biscuit. "I take Aza some food." At the scout's quiet nod, she dips it in the last specks of gravy.

Coming back from visiting Aza, Lakisha spies the kitchen door still ajar. Cook Jennifer carries two small plates. Lakisha's mouth waters with the new smell.

Cook sets one in front of Asante. And another for Lakisha. Flaky white crust sits in a golden mix. The smell of warm peaches fills Lakisha's nose. Looking up for permission, at cook's nod she digs in. The first sweet mouthful melts in her mouth. Sugar, peach and flaky dough. *Heaven*.

Asante takes a small forkful. His mouth quirks into a smile. "Peach?"

Cook Jennifer beams. "First peaches of the

season. Mister scout, how you like my cobbler?"

Asante grasps her hand. "You should come to Kenya with me. The chieftains would make you the royal cook."

Covering her mouth, Jennifer turns in embarrassment and scurries back to the kitchen, tittering.

Savoring the pie, Lakisha looks up at noises from the front room.

Zenobia backs into the dining room. Her hands held up, her robe swirling around her legs. "You can't come in. We are closed—"

An older voice rings out, "I don't care about that. We have to see the Librarian. Now!"

An old lady holding her white shawl tight to her chest has pushed past Zenobia. And a younger woman, in pants and a blue blouse, follows. At Asante's wave, Zenobia retreats, backing out in a hurry. *Lookin' for the Librarian.*

Gripping her shawl tightly, the grey haired one marches on Asante. He puts down his fork, folding his hands, yet calmly, he stays sitting. *He a big man. yet he respectful, like with mama. Don't wan'ta ruffle this ol hen's feathers.*

"You have de librarian's vest on."

Shaking his head. "I am a library scout." His calm steady eyes settle on her and her follower. "From Africa."

"Old Lady." The younger woman puts a hand on the other's arm. "We should not upset the librarians."

"Upset." The old one snatches her arm away. "I'll show 'em upset. I's upset about my farm." She returns Asante's look. "Where 'de Librarian?"

He nods. Respect. "I'm sure the Librarian will

speak to you. Soon."

She holds his gaze for a moment, then relaxes. With a deep breath she watches as he draws her a chair, then sits down. Her eyes never leave Asante.

The younger woman points, to her older companion, still standing, as if her guard. "This be Old Lady Harris. Her farm is being threatened. My mother's farm, the Washington place is also being attacked."

Asante pushes the pie's plate away. "Attacked. Now?"

"By agents!" Old Lady Harris hisses. "With chicanery!"

"Yours are two of the ten farms?"

The old lady gasps. "Ten farms?"

The scout nods. "I heard ten farms are involved." *She didn't know?*

Zenobia returns, behind her the Librarian, also in a robe now.

The lady in blue, still standing gives a little bow. "Librarian?"

Old Lady Harris just hisses again. He looks down at her at his table. Not happy at this disturbance in his evening. "Librarian Oliver. How can I help you?"

The lady clutches at the young woman, who takes over. "We are here for the papers that prove we own our farms."

"Ah. You are from a Gullah farm on Daufuskie Island?"

"We are from two neighboring farms on the island."

"I'm sorry to say there is a problem."

At this a storm moves across the old lady's face. "What you mean? Problem?"

“We have lost the records for ten farms, there.”

She rises, fast as a striking snake, takes a step. Raising her arm. He lifts a hand to ward her off. “We have a plan!”

He points to the scout.

Asante stands now. “I’ll solve this problem, ma’am. I will travel to Beaufort. Fetch copies of the records.”

Old Lady Harris pulls the younger woman close. Her face all but screaming, *Who do I hit. Which one?* But finally that light in her eye dies down a bit. And she offers a nod. “Okay. When you leave?”

“Tomorrow.”

“Okay. Librarians.” Old Lady points to the dining room door. “We leave you. To eat. To sleep. We wait in town.”

The two women share a look, before leaving. But it’s only to the Scout that Old Lady Harris offers, “Thank you.”

6 Farmers United - Warrior

Loud shouting, and general roughhousing comes from out of the bar as Lady Harris and Beneda reach its door. Lady Harris' grandson rises, smiling as soon as he spots Beneda. But she needs to avoid Pete tonight. She asks the old woman, "Where be Jolan. An', Caleb?"

But it's Pete, now at their side, who points into the boisterous room. "Miss Bessie has 'em, wit the others," he shouts, "in da far corner."

"Why you here watching outside?" Old Lady turns her fierce face his way. "Not o'r to the lil' ones?"

"Uh…I's put on the de door." Pete shakes under his gra'ma's scrutiny. "I's keeping people *out*, who's not wit us."

"*Who* put you on de door?" all but bites at him.

Pete lowers his head. "Mister Martin."

She nods at that. "Come Beneda. We see why Martin be orderin' my grandboy about."

The crowd inside is too jumbled to count. Smoke and flickers from oil lamps fill the room. The smell hits her. Booze, sweat, and sawdust. Like breathing through a dirty rag. Up on a table, a man totters and shouts. *There's Martin.* His farm lays to the north of the Washington place. Kids run around off to her far left. Beneda recognizes many faces.

Reaching the dancing fool, Beneda realizes Martin won't be able to hear anything Lady Harris chooses to say. Not waiting to be noticed first by Martin, the old woman grabs a person nearest her; Marquetta.

Pulling Marquetta's head down to her, Lady Harris speaks urgently into her ear. The big girl nods and gets to organizing those around her for Martin's attention. Finally, Martin looks down at all the waving hands, seeing Old Lady Harris.

Creeping to the table's edge, to get him near. His beery expression wars between a nervous smile and belligerence. "Lady Harris!"

"What you monkeyin' about up 'der?"

"Tryin' to get folks' attention!" In frustration, his hands circle the room. "We need to get talkin' on this!"

Old Lady takes in the folk clumped about the room. Beneda's studying them as well, *all arguing 'n shoutin'*.

"Stand up." Old Lady orders. "I' get them t' listen." Obediently he stands a bit straighter on the table, his face showing confusion.

Lady grabs Marquetta again. Then she waves others nearby to come close. Several heads together. "Sing! We singing. *Swing Low*!" The small group starts, then faces outward.

And the hymn begins, Beneda starts softly "Swing low, sweet chariot…" The melody spreads like ripples in water. Soon the room is singing in one honeyed voice. Even the kids stop their fussing to join in.

As the song ends Lady Harris holds a gnarled

hand up high, reaching no higher than Martin's shin. "You'll listen good now. Martin gonna talk about what we gots to do." With people's eyes on her, they quiet some, a few eyes lift to Martin. Beneda studies as people spread the old one's word around the room. Martin, up on the table, waits, holding his arms out.

He looks around. "Folks! We gotta organize." More people pay attention now. "We need to get the information from the Librarians. We need to organize defense of our farms…" He starts, but people near the back still ramble among themselves.

Seeing he's losing the crowd, Martin raises his voice. Pointing to Lady Harris. "Folks! Listen! Lady Harris got to say somethin'. She here when the bad times came. She an' the Washingtons and dems fought to hold our farms then, Listen to her."

People quiet, their focus falls on Lady Harris now.

"I's too old to climb up 'der." She pushes Beneda to the table. Beneda tries resisting, she leans to nearly a sitting position, making herself as small as she can. Tired. But more, she knows she's no talker. "Tell them why we got to fight," whispers Lady Harris. Beneda looks everywhere, at her best friend, Marquetta, then back at the old lady's face. Those serious lines. "Tell dem what dey gots t' lose!"

Deciding, Beneda climbs up in the bench. To help, Martin grabs her wrists and hauls her up to him, like he's still in charge of this all. Now she don't know what to say. She looks around the packed room. *Different up here where you can see all these faces.* Her eyes dart, stopping at faces she recognizes. Focusing only on those she knows, she waves and addresses them one after another.

“Mister Bailey, Missus Hogg, Sandy Gilbert. Y’all know me. Beneda.” She dips her chin, a greeting and a grin. “My grandma defended your farms with this bow.” She touches a fingertip to it on her back. “As M’Deah would say, *A gladi foh si une.”* A roar fills the room at the Gullah. “If’n M’Deah was here, she tell you we needs t’ work t’gether.”

All these faces looking up. Shining in the smoky light. “If’n we don’t work as one. We *all* lose our farms. Where our grandmas and grandpapas be buried.” Tears role down her cheeks, and not from the table’s height or the fear of speaking up this way. “Help me save our farm,” she calls, and in response, the room shakes with holler’n. She steps down. Unsteady.

Many hands reaching up to help.

Beneda looks back up to the table. Martin has his arm raised again. Tryin’ to get back the attention. “Please. Everyone pick one person. Each farm. Meet me and Lady Harris! T’ plan.” Looking at those bright faces, Martin adds, “Us and Beneda Washington.”

~~~

The ten men and women around the bar table lean closer to hear each other.

“Okay. We agree then.” Martin proclaims loudly. “Mos’ us head back to our farms.” He continues after the nods round the table, reciting off his fingers, “We organize—shared defense at home. Old Willy teach us. Him served in the army as a youngun.” The explaining means he gets to say more, and Martin, he does, looking eye to eye, face to face. Like he be back up shoutin’ on that table. “Come to each others’ aid, if attacked.” Martin, shoulder hunched and elbows all
~~~

tight, instructs, "A few will stay here and check up on the Librarians."

Lady Harris grasps Beneda's wrist. "Gots to light a fire under dem Librarians."

Beneda nods, and promises her, "I visit de library come morning."

As they break up, Beneda looks for Jolan. Sees he over by Pete and the others. Making her way over is slow. Many pats and *atta girl* from the people she passes. A loud shout draws her eye. Miss Bessie points an' yells at a man.

Moving closer, Beneda hears Miss Bessie. "He don't belong here. Ain't one of us."

His arms up. Nice clothes. Very clean jacket. No spots on his pants. Trying to quiet the shouter. "I work a nearby farm." But Beneda sees him sidle back. Something about that. "Turner, from the Brown farm, he done told me about de meetin'." His eye dart around. "I'm Cootuh." he scurries left, headed to the door. Giving up just that quick. Miss Bessie, she *harumphs* the man on his way.

That Miss Bessie, she turn a cow bent on headin' for a stream. Beneda notices Pete, come to get on her next nerve. But he may have news. He was given the kids. And after all, as the Old Lady be telling Beneda all the way here, *Pete cain't be helpin' his feelings*.

"Pete." She sees Jolan is not missing her at all. He be with Caleb and the other lil'uns. Maybe he startin' to tire.

"Beneda." Pete smiles. "I gots a room for you and Jolan." He hangs his head, like his shoes be asking some question.

"What?" *He done something wrong?*

Pete keeps those eyes down. “Caleb ask ta stay with you all.” Hesitating. “I say yes.”

Beneda thought it was going to be a problem. A problem with Pete. “That okay. They c’n entertain theyselves. Boys need that ev’ry once an a while.” Pete nods. And thinking about the next morning, she tells him, “Early day. We best go now.”

Rounding up Jolan and Caleb takes time. Beneda bides with Marquetta. She hugs Beneda. “You speak so well, girl.” Beneda dips her head. Embarrassed. “Now, people will look to you to lead.”

Beneda thinks about her friend’s words. *What’s goin’ happen next.* “Lots of trouble fuh alla us.” Marquetta, she just nods.

“Caleb stayin’ wit us!” Jolan runs up, grabbing at Beneda’s hand.

“I heard. Let’s go.” Beneda holds his hand tight.

“Aw.” Tries to tug away. Jolan calls from Beneda’s grip, “Caleb! We goin’!”

Pete pulls Caleb over. They herd the two lil’uns like fractious calves. Out the door. Beneda can’t see in the dark street. Moon must be at the near new.

“Dis way.” Pete pulls Caleb. Good, Pete can lead them. “It close. Just two doors away.”

“Good.” Beneda holds Jolan tight. “I’d get lost.”

Once in the lobby of the large inn, Pete leads them right past the front desk to the stairs. “In de middle, the top floor.” He pauses on the top step. “Old Lady and I be on first floor.” Beneda does not want to ask for a favor. But she must.

Stopping at a door. Pete bows, “It’s here.” Opening the door, he pushes Caleb in. Jolan follows all in a scramble, then Pete seizes Beneda's hand.

Pulling away, she busies that hand with the knob and doorsill. Prim. She lowers her lashes, and says only, "Pete. Please come by early. You need to take Caleb and Jolan for the day." He seems a little upset at that but she's plowing on, "I'ma going to see the librarians. Early." She steps back to door. Grabbing the knob to pull it tight if need be.

As she closes it, she hears, "Yes, Beneda…"

7 Journeys - Warrior

It's the smell of sassafras Beneda wakes to. Thinking of mama, her glance travels around this small room. Jolan and Caleb lie entwined on the pallet in the corner. Soft boyish snores coming up from the floor. Arms flung across they chests like pups. On the table beside her bed, steam rises from a ceramic cup. *Ah. Pete's been in here.*

Up and ready in a few minutes, she tugs at the blanket under the boys to wake them. They rise slowly as boys are wont to, complaining and groaning.

"Get ready," Beneda calls. "I fin' t' leave in a few minutes."

Jolah straightens his shirt, scratches at he head. "I never seen a library!"

"You stay'n with Pete." At his scowl, Beneda takes that breath you do with the young. Holding back what most woulda done with a switch, or a cuff and a curse. "An' Caleb. He be wit'cha." That calms the young one. Some.

"Ah." Jolan grips the handle of his knife. "You might need protect'n"

Patting his head, she orders, "You protect Old Lady Harris."

She turns at the door's opening. Sounds from downstairs wash in with Pete. He waves another in.

Marquetta, from the Hogg place. Her quick twists for braids frame her face. *What kinda friend am I? She need to come to me this early a'morning.*

"Pete." Beneda greets him. "Thanks for the tea." Taking a sip, and examining the other young woman's new dress. "Marquetta…"

Pete reaches and gets one of the two boys, but the other snatches his shoulder away right quick. "I brought Marquetta to accompany you."

Well, Marquetta *is* one of the strongest on the farms. "Okay. Let's go." Inspecting the boys. They seem decent. "Jolan, you behave. See you soon."

Jolan squirms. Trying to escape Pete's grip. "'kay. Hurry."

With a wave, Beneda summons Marquetta and closing the door behind, they leave the boys to Pete.

Marquetta, she catches up at the stairs. "Girl. Why don'cha give that young man somma yo time?"

Rolling her eyes, Beneda snaps back. "Don't have time. Now."

Making their way out to street. Beneda's shoulder takes on a stiffer pose. The town's come to life this morning. The early light still casts shadows toward the west. Beneda doesn't recognize anyone of the bustling locals. But faces, like those from last night's meeting, smile from here and there on the street.

Marquetta starts up again. "If'n you don't spare the time, some other woman'll beat yours." At this, Beneda walks faster. Marquetta, she a big girl, she easily keeps up. "He not good enough for you? Someday, he be the man of the Harris place."

Beneda slows. Each syllable clear, rimmed with frost, "You are quite welcome to try."

"Girl. What wrong with him? You'all once was

thick as thieves."

"Maybe that's the problem. Growin' up t'gether. I seen him all my life. He only look fresh n' new to you."

That finally shuts Marquetta up. Well, kinda,"Aw, Beneda…"

And it's only three more blocks to go in the silence that follows.

Beneda sees the Bluffton Library just a block away. The four white stone pillars up to the roofline reflecting the sun. She hopes to catch the scout before he leaves for Beaufort.

Entering the marbled lobby her eyes light on the same gatekeeper as the previous day. A look of panic flits over the woman's face. Then calmness takes over. Slowly rising from her chair, her robe swirling in the dappled light, the woman's smile increases, seeing as Old Lady hasn't accompanied these ladies this morning.

"Miss Beneda?" She tries, genteel as all gatekeepers are.

Beneda gives a little bow. "I seek the scout. Has he left yet?"

The woman's lips quirk. "You are just in time. You and…"

"Marquetta. Miss."

"Zenobia." She gestures to a bench against the wall. "You are both welcome to wait, the lobby's cool. We'll leave the door ajar for a breeze. The scout will be out shortly."

Surveying the woman's desk, Beneda makes a request of the sharply dressed assistant, "Miss Zenobia. Could I have a sheet of paper? I want to write to my mother."

After a brief pause, Zenobia waves the girl over to a chair near her own desk. "Here you are." Holding a sheet out, she finds a pen and sets it out as well, with soft, pale hands.

Sitting straighter, Beneda thanks her. Marquetta, she plops down on the bench across the room, stares out the big window as if something of interest waits out there. As Beneda examines the pen nib, Zenobia unscrews an inkwell. Handling the paper, Beneda feels its rough grain on the beige sheet.

Dipping the pen, she points to the paper. "Made here?"

"Yes, we mold a batch every month," comes Zenobia surprised answer.

Beneda nods, composing an account of the events in town for her mama. Covering the problem in a quick, tight hand, with the records and the decision of the farmers; she concludes quickly.

Handing the pen back, she bows again. "Thank you, Zenobia." Blowing on the page, she lifts it and stands.

Marquetta asks from across the wide room, "Givin' it to Jolan?"

Beneda shakes it gently, folds it and secrets it in her pack. "He can take it to Mama."

A barefooted girl, entering silently from a back room, stops this exchange. Beneda recognizes her from last night. The girl with the scout.

The girl approaches the receptionist. "Miss Zenobia. Please. This letter for my mama. In Port Wentworth."

Zenobia inspects the address written there. "Yes, Lakisha. I can add it to the regular mail pack sent out today." She slips it into a stack of things on the corner of her desk and smiles her gatekeeper smile all around.

"Thanks ma'am."

Beneda is about to speak, but then the scout steps into the room, *Ah, Yes.* There's a pack in his hand. His sword's strapped on. Her heart jumps up to her throat. A dog at his side, nails *click-clicking* on the polished floor. It sits, examines Beneda, then Marquetta.

"Aza. Wait outside." With one glance up at the scout's face, the dog trots out through the propped open wide front door. Noise from the road drifts in from outside.

Beneda bows to the scout, practices her start. But then stops. She lets herself breathe out, before trying again, *I gotta do this here right*. "Scout Asante." Her best voice rings in the lobby, "I wanted a word with you."

The tall scout's smile warms her like the sun. "You are Beneda. From a farm?"

"Yes, Sir." Beneda's head bobs. Half bow, half nervous twitch, she feels Marquetta behind her, watching. Judging every move, the girl watches, waiting. "I wanted to inquire—when you expecting to return?"

Marquetta speaks up, "The families want to know."

The big man nods all around, even to the library worker. "Yes. I understand. Well…" he looks to the young girl. "I hope to be back late tomorrow night." There's a smile there, no dithering at all. "Lakisha. What do you think?"

The girl looks doubtful, touches the edge of that big desk, something in her eyes flicks before she says,

“Maybe.”

Beneda tries a smile. She doesn’t have exactly what she wants, but, she wants this scout to remember her well. Her words come from a place of satisfaction now, Marquetta shifting and waiting. “Thank you. Mister scout. I hope you have a pleasant, and successful journey.”

“Asante.” A hand rises to his chest, then two hands come together, adding to his bow to the ladies, one and all, even Marquetta, who titters. “And I hope to have the answer that will help your family.” He reaches a hand out to Lakisha. “Let’s get on the road.” Looking back. “Hope to see you soon.”

Marquetta hurries over and grabs Beneda’s arm. “Hopes to see *you* soon—”

“—shut up.” Beneda acts like maybe Zenobia could post her letter too, but that’s just a stall. She mimes a bit, and then makes a show of changing her mind. And finally the pair heads for the door.

Marquetta hurries to keep up with her old friend. “Think you could find any time for *him*?”

~~~

A crowd of farmers mill about on the street, as Beneda and Marquetta near the bar.

“Why you come with me this mornin’, Marquetta?”

“It was Pete. He talk to me.” She waves. “You be important now.” The farmers ahead wave back, some nod like they two’s something special all of a sudden. “We have to protect you.”

Beneda shakes her head, it rattles her bow and quiver on her back. *Not me.* “I’m not no one.”

Marquetta snickers. “Even library scouts hope to
~~~

see *you* soon." Beneda pushes her fleshy shoulder. Jolan runs up.

"Beneda." He calls, "Why you cain't come wit us?"

Beneda pulls out the letter. Handing it over. Fixing her eyes on the boy's, her voice drops, this be serious as a heart attack and Jolan needs to get that straight in his mind. "I gots to stay. A few more days. You take this to my mama." Into his small pack it goes. Hands on his shoulders, stern, she schools the child, "Don't lose it!"

"Okay. But, me n' Caleb—"

"—I mean it now." And Jolan stills. Nodding. Just the smallest of jiggles to his feet now.

"Yep. Yas'um. But when you com'n back?"

"Soon. A few days. I'ma see Old Lady. Get ready to leave." She straightens, gets Lady Harris' attention from the crowd.

The older woman reaches out for Beneda's hand, seems to send some message in that grip. "You see the Librarian?"

"I talked to the scout. He be off to Beaufort, now. Thinks he be back tomorrow night."

Lady Harris shifts her pack on her shoulder. "Good. Send us word. Soon's you hear." She waves to the knot of farmers milling around on the sidewalk planks. "Turner from Brown's place has a horse."

Beneda nods. *Turner. He gots de horse*. Her list.

Martin's shouting to get folks' attention. "We're leaving!" Stepping out, several follow him closely, eastbound. Others tarry, get organized slower, but all finally straggle onto the road. Near forty kilometers to home.

First Beneda hugs Lady Harris then pats Jolan on

the back to hurry him along. He grabs Caleb's hand and skips off to join the group. Lady Harris takes a place at the end of the crowd. Snatching at one of the more loud and riley litt'uns. Then Pete approaches.

"Beneda. Wanted to talk to you."

"Yes, Pete."

Giving her a bent smile, shy about his words, he begins, "Wanted t' see more of you this trip—"

Beneda ducks her head. *Be honest. Be nice.* "It's been bedlam." Marquetta, she come walking over. But, seeing Pete, turns into the bar, quick on her feet for such a wide gal.

"Yes. Fer sure." His eyes drop to his feet. *Nervous?* "What about when you get back?"

Knowing what he wants. "Maybe." She means *no*. But, cain't say it.

His smile straightens. "Thanks! I see you then!" He half-turns, smiling even bigger, then turns the rest of the way and hurries to catch up with the walking group. Marquetta slides back out the bar's door.

"Beneda." Marquetta laughs. "I get back home, I'ma tell your mama what you doin' t' all these menfolk."

~~~

"We can't show our faces again at home!" Marquetta slams her cup down on the table. Beneda rears back. A wet sloppy mess speckles her top.

Raising his hands, Turner firmly answers the big girl. "I just say'n'…" He takes in the others around the table. "We needa be ready. If the news be bad."

"Won't have no bad news, Turner!" Marquetta snaps back. "Beneda's African gonna bring us what we need."
~~~

Beneda frowns lightning bolts at Marquetta, not yet matching the girl, drink for drink. “He’s not *my* African.”

Marquetta puts on a silly grin. She got what she wanted. “He said, *he hoped to help you.*” The other two at the table stare at Beneda now. Knowing she’s toting her bow and quiver. And that she don’t play. “Kunte, was that his name?”

Beneda tries a kick under the table. “Asante!” She tries not rising to Marquetta’s bait. Her voice comes down in pitch, “Asante, is his name.”

“Oh. Yeah. What did *Asante* say?” Marquetta’s silly cocked grin mocks her.

Miss Bessie interrupts their game. “Whatever we hear. We will report back to our farms.”

Letting it go, Marquetta nods across the table. “Turner. You ready of a ride back?”

Turner takes a slow sip. “My horse be ready.”

Beneda stands. “We done?” At the nods. “I’ma get some air.”

Marquetta stands too, the lady, now her mouth’s done its wickedness. “Yes. I’ll join you.”

Beneda ignores her, making her way through the mostly empty bar to the door. Outside the May sun is beating down bright and hot. As they step outside, she tries to ignore her tipsy friend.

Dogging Beneda’s steps out into the dusty street, Marquetta tries for appeasing, “You’re the leader now.”

Shaking her head, Beneda focuses up and down the street. She squints at the busy town, strangers headed who knows where. “You keep saying that.”

“It true.” Marquetta waves back into the bar. To Miss Bessie and Turner, still in town. “With all the older folks gone, we all look to you."

Beneda gives in. "Fine." Another head shake. Slower this time, she admits, "I wish I knew how to help."

Marquetta puts on her impish grin again. "You just gots t' motivate de right mens to get us what we need."

Beneda is about to snap at her, but notices a figure in a familiar robe approaching from the library's direction. Grabs Marquetta's arm, and points. Marquetta follows her finger and squeals low, conspiring. "Hey. She from the library!"

"Yes. Zenobia."

The exquisitely dressed woman stops in front of the pair. "Miss Beneda."

With a small bow. "Miss Zenobia. You looking for me?"

"I have a letter for you. From the Librarian." She taps a spot on her robe's sleeve.

Beneda guesses nobody would want to discuss library business on the street. "The bar?"

Marquetta, quick girl that she is, shakes her head, and advises, "You'll not avoid the others."

Zenobia nods.

Right. "My room." Beneda points down the street. She ushers the women two doors down, like she'd been born to take the lead.

She feels like apologizing for the mess. "I see the boys left their blankets spread on the floor." Her near empty tea cup sits on the table by the unmade bed. As she turns back to Zenobia, Marquetta rushes past gathering things up in both hands. Tossing the blankets in the corner, her sure hands then set to straightening up the bed. Calmly, Zenobia judges something in Beneda's face. A decision is made and the Librarian's helper is pulling a page from the folds of her robe. "I have this for you."

Beneda examines the paper. More mold-pressed, by the library, thick and rich. Red wax seals its edge. Marquetta produces a knife. Taking it, Beneda slits the seal open. She again admires the paper, opening and reading the single page.

Zenobia remains planted near the doorway. "I was told to wait. If you had a response." A pen has appeared from another of those sleeve's folds.

Beneda's knees shake as she finishes reading. Marquetta reaches for her in alarm. But Beneda shakes her head, remaining upright. Reading the letter again.

"There can be no response to this." Her words sharper than she intends. At both women's shocked expressions, Beneda hands the page to Marquetta.

Her head down, a moment, mouth moving line to line, Marquetta hands tremble. Looking up at the library worker with fire in her eyes. "You know what's in here?"

Zenobia takes a step back. "No. The Librarian bade me only to bring it to Miss Beneda."

Beneda lays a restraining hand on Marquetta, she lets the messenger know what it was she's delivered, "Librarian Oliver suggests it might be better for the farmers to sell their farms."

Zenobia's brows arch up; she takes in a quick gasp. "I had no—I did not know." Her hand wipes away this news of the message, a pushing movement, a step closer to the door. "He sealed it."

Marquetta ignores her now. Thrusting the letter back into Beneda's hands, asking, "What you gon' tell de others?"

Beneda bites her lip. Hard. "I can't tell them. This." Looking at Zenobia. "I have to talk to the Librarian."

Zenobia nods. "I'll take you to him."

Marquetta looks around the room. Checking it's straightened. "What you want me do?"

In thought, Beneda raises her eyes to the ceiling. *Everyone looks to you,* echoes for a second. "Don't tell the others." Handing her bow and quiver to Marquetta. "Give me a chance to talk this out." She gestures to Zenobia and they head out the door.

"I be right back." Beneda calls, "Meet you at the bar." Her mind's wriggling like a snake. Will Asante help the farmers?

Behind them Marquetta stands on the open doorway, her call following them down the hall, "The librarians have to help!"

Beneda ignores people passing on the street. What will she say to Librarian Oliver? He needs to understand, only way her farmers will leave their land is dead.

A flash to the side grabs her eye. Two shapes coming out the alley. Beneda pushes Zenobia back, sliding the letter into the gatekeeper's hand as a dusty, musk smell hits her. She reaches down, for her knife in her boot, but hasn't the seconds to touch it. Darkness covers her eyes. A bag. Onion smell. Burlap. Her feet come off the ground in an instant. Zenobia's scream cut off quickly, with a squishy thud.

8 African Scout - Heart

Lakisha and the scout stand back as a four-horse coach slows to a stop. The driver looks down at them, eyes the vest Asante wears. Raising his hat a fraction off his head, he asks, “Librarian. Where you bound?”

“Beaufort.” Asante shades his eyes. “Libraries’ business.”

“I’d appreciate having another weapon aboard. Hop on.” He waves below. “The stages been attacked by robbers in these parts.”

As Asante opens the coach door, Lakisha glances at the man sitting up top beside the driver. A large man, holding a staff between his knees.

Lakisha’s thinking, *Nice. Fine lookin’ in there. But I should be ridin’ top of the stage. Not with these folks.* But the Scout takes her elbow, and she’s up on the first step into the coach. Moving in, Lakisha takes one of the empty front seats. A well-dressed older man and woman sit opposite.

In for a penny, in for a pound. “Up here, Aza,” Lakisha calls. And the dog jumps in next, stretching out at her feet. The other riders appear calm, they watch, not worried by Aza or her, close to their clean shoes.

Asante climbs in, planting himself next to Lakisha. She compares his sandals to the man’s leather shoes. The sandals are well traveled, the shoes new.

"I am Lakisha. This is Asante, library scout." Said with pride. "That is Aza."

The well-dressed man nods at the tidy woman to his right. "My wife, Savannah." Of himself, he says, "Doctor Isaac. We are the Chasseurs of Beaufort." His glance is on Asante. "Sir."

Asante gives a small bow. "Pleased to make your acquaintance."

Savannah, the wife, speaks up. "That accent. From where do you hail, Mister Asante?"

"From Kenya, by way of Sierra Leone."

Her eyes light and she nods at this. Her husband responds, "Savannah ran an article in the Beaufort Gullah Times last year about African roots. Highlighting that aspect of our life here in the Lowcountry." Asante smiles. Probably in appreciation, Lakisha figures. As this Dr. Chasseur of Beaufort explains, "She owns and runs that newspaper." Proud of his wife.

She pats her man's arm. "My bragging husband should tell you he is well respected in town, and for miles outside it."

Asante bows, "I am indeed honored to share a coach with such notables."

Lakisha's impressed. Never known doctors or newspaper women. The woman hides her smile.

~~~

Waking, Lakisha feels the coach slow. Craning she looks forward out the small squares of window, left and right, but she's facing backward and doesn't see much for why they might stop here.
~~~

“Log in the road.” Comes a call from above.

As the coach stops, the driver calls down. “Trouble!”

Asante stands, He directs Lakisha, “Stay here. Out of sight.” He nods to the couple.

The coach creaks and sways as overhead the driver and guard climb down. Lakisha can’t help peeking out the small window.

Freeing his sword, and striding from the coach, Asante asks, “Can we back up?”

But the driver shakes his head. Pulls a long knife out. Bowie knife. “That’ll take too long. If’n someone comes.”

“Aza. There.” The scout’s hand extends toward the rear of the coach. Lakisha can’t see the guard. Must be on de other side.

Leaves shake as men stride onto the road. Lakisha sees four from her vantage point, low at the coach’s window. One big, darker than the others, with a sword. A shorter one, with a bow. Lakisha thinks, *Cain’t be more’n a few years older ’n me*. A third holds a club, but not like he knows to use it. And the last, a thinner one, grips a sword.

Asante flicks his hand. Lakisha’s eyes move to Aza’s creeping shape. The dog slowly pads, low to the ground, rounding behind the men. The bowman shifts his aim between the stage-men, Asante, and the dog to his side.

That big sword flashes, held by the leader of this quartet. In a leather vest. Dirty from top to bottom. Black sandals. And that huge sword.

“Drop your weapons!” He waves his at the driver. “Give us your valuables. No one gets hurt.”

The driver shakes his head. “We can’t do that.”

He looks to the guard, coming up on his right, and over to Asante. “Leave now, and we’ll let you go.”

The big bandit laughs. His other men smile. All but the young archer, trying to decide which of the four to aim at.

“You don’t want to fight us.” A rough laugh leaves his lips. “Robbed five coaches this spring,” the bandit boasts, “One guarded by deputies. Not a scratch!”

Asante raises his sword, Slowly. Straight up. It glints. When everyone is looking at him. He calls out, “This stage is under the protection of the libraries.” His head moves from one bandit to the next.

Aza crouches, still. Tensed. Less than a meter behind the archer’s hamstrings. “On library business. Stop us, and there is nowhere you can hide.” He again swivels his head, eyes locking on each bandit in turn. “The libraries can track you across this continent. And any other.”

Club man shifts his weapon, from left to right. “Sam?”

The boss gives an angry scowl at the fool. “No names!” This leader looks back at Asante. At that sword straight up in the air. At the driver’s long knife. The guard’s staff. And then back to Aza. Quiet and still.

Lakisha watches, breath on her throat, *Mebbe he counting*.

“Okay.” He addresses the driver. “You all lucky, this time. Next time you pay a toll.”

Turning, the men walk away. Hardly a backward glance. In a moment they’ve disappeared. Melted into the trees like wind into a swamp.

~~~
~~~

Stay awake. Lakisha thinks to herself, *why fear make a body so sleepy?* They near Beaufort, surely. The doctor, his wife, and Asante have talked for hours. Only Aza and Lakisha are quiet.

A voice comes from above, “Five minutes to Beaufort!”

With a frown, the doctor, Chasseur, asks the scout, “How long will you be in our town?”

Shaking his head, Asante spreads his hands. “Probably not more than a day. Picking up papers and returning to Bluffton.”

Doctor Chasseur grasps his wife’s gloved hand gently. “Too bad. I was going to invite you to dine with us. It’s been too long, finding such interesting conversation; science, world travel, astronomy, mathematics.”

“Thank you. Perhaps another time?”

With the stage slowing, the passengers crane their necks to see out the small windows. Lakisha spies a few houses and people walking.

As the horses snort and blow and the stage stops, the driver calls, “Librarian! You will want to get off here.” Asante reaches over and opens the door. “The library is just two streets over.” He points with his whip. “On Scott.”

Lakisha stands and stretches, remembering about bowing to the doctor and his wife.

“Pleased to meet you, Lakisha.” Missus Chasseur smiles.

Nodding nervously Lakisha jumps down. “Aza. Come.” Aza stretches into a play bow, sparing a glance at the passengers before jumping himself.

Asante bows his head. He calls up, “I have

enjoyed our time together."

The doctor nods. "We too. Here's to meeting again."

As the scout holds out a hand to help her down, Lakisha notes the driver is writing with a torn paper and nub of a pencil.

He calls down. "Librarian. What be your name?"

"Asante. Scout Asante."

"Me an' Malachi are thankful for your help back there." Wiping sweat off his brow he holds the scrap of paper up. "In payment, here is a note telling whatever driver you meet to offer up a ride."

The scout bows and reaches up. "Thank you. Kindly of you to drop us so close."

With a stretch, the driver hands it down. Then with a tap on the brim of his hat to Lakisha, he offers a second smile. "Goodbye, Miss." With a flick of his wrist, the team starts forward. Lakisha slams the door quickly and waves to the passengers as they move away, another number of blocks for them to go to the stage-line station.

It's bright out of the stage. And moving with the river behind them, Lakisha recognizes some houses. From the time she was here with her mother. "I never been to the library. But, I been near here."

The scout's scanning the neighborhood. "Where are we?"

"I been to Pigeon Point Park." She points north. "Just up a ways, up beside the Harbor River."

Asante waves at a brick building. "I think we are here."

Lakisha gapes at the long low building to the right, even bigger than Bluffton's. "Will they expect us?"

"Librarian Oliver said he would send a pigeon."

Cocking her head. "Pigeon?"

Asante casts a smile down at his guide. "Librarian Oliver informed me that pigeons are used to send messages between the libraries in this area."

"Huh! I wants to see dat!"

Crossing the square before the library's door, Aza leads them, his doggy nails clicking on the brick leading to the entrance.

Beside the huge arched window, Lakisha focuses on a young man, sitting behind a desk.

"Scout Asante?" At the scout's nod, the young man touches his open book, "We know of your mission. I believe Librarian Lincoln has papers for you." He stands.

Lakisha, Aza and the scout wait in the dusky glow coming through the large floor to ceiling window, weary, quiet as they sit. In moments the young man returns with a woman in that distinctive vest. "Librarian Lincoln, Scout Asante and companions," he announces before returning to his desk.

"Welcome, Scout Asante." She bows. As he returns a bow of his own, the Librarian's eyes crinkle, as she smiled to Lakisha. "Hello little one, you must be the guide I heard about."

Lakisha bows, looking down at her feet, at Aza's wiggly tail. "Yas'um. I'm Lakisha, Ma'am."

The librarian points down at the pup, sitting at attention beside the scout's sandals. "And, who is this?"

Lakisha pats his head. "This be Aza. He from Africa."

"Good boy, Aza." She calls the clerk back, "Can

we perhaps get our guests some fruit?" With a wave, she turns to business, and steps to a side room, beckoning the Scout. "Come. I have what you have journeyed for."

Entering the smaller room Lakisha spies a table laid out with water and cups. She crooks her finger to Aza and offers a cup of water for him. Filling two more, she carries them over to Asante to hand him one.

"Thank you." He points at a bag on the wooden desk that the librarian stands beside. "The land deeds?"

"Yes, we have made copies." She pulls a pile of paper partway out of the bag. Shaking her head with a small frown. "Our scribes can't copy the official seals on the documents. These will not serve in a court case. But, you can understand we don't want to let the originals out of our hands."

Asante bows and reaches for the bag. "I understand. I suspect merely having the copies will convince people." The clerk enters, with a bowl of fruit.

The librarian seems a bit preoccupied, Lakisha can see the set of her shoulders. But she only tells the scout, "Yes. Or, they may take drastic action." She glances at Lakisha, then at Aza busy at the cup set down for him. *Thinking we be a strange group?* "Already, Bluffton is sounding too exciting."

Asante cocks his head. "Why is that?"

The librarian then points to her desk, where a thin bit of paper lies curled. "A few minutes ago, a second pigeon from Bluffton arrived. A farmer girl has been kidnapped."

The scout looks at Lakisha. Aza glances up at his

master's face. "Does it say who?"

Librarian Lincoln's finger traces down the much curled message. Asante's big hands knead the cloth sack with the deeds.

"Why, yes." Her eyes scan the thin page. "Beneda Washington." She looks up at the scout's face. "Do you know of her?"

He bites his lip. "Yes. We've met her. Twice. At the Bluffton Library." He glances down at Lakisha. And the dog. "How fast can I leave?"

The librarian rubs her face, considering. "You are in luck." She looks over to a tall floor clock, she thinks a loud, "Five minutes to six. Well, twice a week there's a night stage to Bluffton." Taking a step to the door. "Preston!" she calls once more.

The young man hurries in. "Yes, Librarian?"

"Quick. Run to the stage line. Tell them to wait the stage to Bluffton." She examines the three travelers. "Tell them a library scout will be there in ten minutes. Go now!"

Without a word, the young man turns and trots out, Aza's ears lift, but he stays at the scout's feet. She turns back to her desk. "Are you ready. Do you need anything?" Asante shakes his head. She takes Lakisha's arm and aims her back to the table. "Take the fruit, child. Take it all. You've probably missed a meal on the ride over."

Asante's taps on the Librarian's desk, his mind on more than fruit. "Librarian, may I send a message via your pigeon to Librarian Oliver at Bluffton."

Nodding, Lincoln she points to the pen and well and moves behind her desk to draw out a new thin sheet from a cubbyhole. Asante sets down his extra bag, sitting for a moment, he then writes. In a moment he's blowing on the page, handing it to the woman.

Holding the fine sheet of paper, Librarian Lincoln beckons them back into the main room. The others follow, Lakisha now with fruit weighing down her bag.

Calling into a connecting room, "Annebelle!" A woman walks out in an apron, flour sprinkles dotting it.

"Yes, Miss Lincoln?"

"Annebelle, can you please take these travelers to the stage line." At the cook's nod. She explains, "I've sent Preston to hold the Bluffton stage. They need to catch the night coach."

"Yas'um. I'll get 'em right there."

"Will we get there in time to help?" Lakisha looks up at the scout, wondering.

9 Lost Freedom - Warrior

Learn names, make friends, stay alive, Beneda lists her priorities. What she needs to do. The burlap covering her head lets in little light, but not much air.

"I am Beneda Washington…" Her muffled voice fills her head in the sack. Wriggling her hands can't free them. Rough twine irritates her wrists. As she tries to stand, a big hand pushes down on her shoulder. Unwashed human smell attacks her nose.

"Sit down!" That voice. The red-headed club wielder on her farm. *Baldy is probably around as well, damn his eyes.*

What can make them worry? She gasps for more breath. "The librarians are involved!" That smell. "You don't want to fight them over me."

A gruff laugh comes from the left. Small room, maybe. *A barn, or shed?* "We ain't scairt o' no *libaryuns*."

The bald one? Yes. Must be.

Sounds of a door, behind her, draws her attention. Sounds on each side. *Are these two brutes snapping to attention?*

"Hey!" Beneda hears this new voice. "Take that that thing offa her head." Good. She will be able to identify them. To testify.

Squinting her eyes against the sudden brightness, Beneda sees only shadows.

"We gots her like you said." The red-head. "Mister Cootuh. Jus' like you said." She's heard that name. *Where?*

"I apologize for my over-enthusiastic friends." That voice also. It comes to her in a rush. The bar, at the meeting. "Miss Washington, please accept my apologies. They be rough men. Not gentlefolk, like us."

His face comes into focus. Clean clothes. *Yes, Cootuh. From the bar*. "You're a farmer, sir? From our meeting?"

His head ducks. "Sorry, Miss. I stretched the truth." Looking at Red-head. "Those ropes are unnecessary. She a lady, after all."

The big man shambles closer, grumbles. "Yes, Mister Cootuh." Kinda like a big puppy. A big scary puppy.

Beneda schools herself not to flinch. Reminds herself of her list of priorities. *Make friends, stay alive.*

"I ain't actually a farmer." The gentleman apologizes again. "But, I work for people interested in buying yuh land."

"This ain't the way to do it." Beneda's tone is fierce. Red-head works on untying her. Beneda holds her breath.

"Please forgive me." Cootuh's head bows. "I thought if'n we talked…you could see my point of view—"

"—Release me!" Beneda interrupts.

"Soon, I promise." He sets a hand on his chest, like that matters. "We can talk together to your farmer friends."

Beneda takes a few breaths. With free hands, now

the red-headed one has stepped back, she rubs her wrists and wonders how do deal with these *agents*. She focuses on how to win. For her mother. For the farm. And adjusts her tone, two can be heartfelt. "Your boss should write down his demands."

A smile breaks across the smooth one's face. "Bring Miss Washington some water." Red-head steps to a dusty table and from a banged up jug he pours. "My employees wish to remain anonymous. You understand. They be so tender-hearted, it might could upset them."

The water. Beneda thanks the thug with as genuine a smiles as she can muster, *learn names*. And takes a sip; thinking furiously. "Thank you— " She halts, looking to the smooth one, an eyebrow raised.

"He be Brutha, Miss." Cootuh offers, "Just Brutha."

"Thank you— *Brutha* —she then tells this smooth one, "I can take your demands to my fellow farmers."

Another smile. The dandy makes an exaggerated bow at that smile. "Excellent." Then frowns, a shadow flits across his brow. "But, best we wait for nightfall. Don't want no chance 'a getting caught."

Satisfied at that thought, nodding to the two toughs, he addresses her again. "Wait here with my friends. Don't cause them no trouble. Or, they will have to tie you again. I'll return with the dusk."

~~~

The big red-head, Brutha growls at Beneda, "You be lucky Mister Cootuh say not ta' hurt you."

The slick one, Cootuh, had seemed patient and harmless. But this one…
~~~

With a disgusted look, he turns to the bald one. "Hector. You stay. I'ma go to town. Gets us somfin t' eat."

Eagerly, his partner blurts, "Okay. You go."

This Hector, a simple one.

Brutha stomps out, calling back, "An' watch her!"

Hector looks from the slamming door to Beneda in the chair.

Swinging her foot out so it snaps the binding against the chair leg, she asks, "Hector?" Her voice low and slow, "Untie my foot… please?"

Hector again glances at the door. "I best not." His eyes run from her shoulders down to her shoes. Thinking a minute, he then asks, "You promise not to run off?"

Beneda bites her lip. "I can't. My momma be wait'n for me. Back to the farm."

He shuffles over the table. "You want some water?"

Beneda reminds herself, *be friendly*. "Yes. Please." He holds a cup out to her, and she risks, "Does your momma know what you doing here?"

Hector's face shows confusion at this. "Ain't seem my momma in years." Shaking his head, he points to the door. "Brutha take care'a me. Fer years."

He'd do it, if I ask just the right way. "You *should* help Brutha." She holds the cup to her lips, looking at him with wide opened eyes. Like she's been startled by a frog.

"Brutha don't need help." Again, Hector's eyes slide to the door. "He get'n us food."

Lowering the cup, keeping her eyes still wider, she ventures, "How you gonna help him, when he in jail?"

Cocking his head. "He ain't going to *jail.*" The word rising. Almost a question.

"Sure is." She shakes her head, a bit of sorrow in her voice, but more a scolding momma. "You both goin'."

"No—"

"Oh, yes." Putting on a stern look. "You know what you done?" At his blank look, she presses him like a teacher would. "Y'all kidnapped me. Authorities will be looking. Librarians. Right quick, too."

In defiance, Scrunching his face, Hector boasts, repeating, "We ain't scairt'a no *libaryuns*."

"You brave now…" Beneda holds the cup toward the frail wooden door. "How you be when they come bustin' that in?"

Hector stares at the door, like it's just spoke. *What can make it scarier?* "You know the punishment for kidnapping?" Pausing, like a stage player. "Life at hard labor. Them chain gangs mean you never get out."

With a thin quivery voice, Hector keeps up the bravery, "I ain't scairt!"

It's then that Beneda twists the knife. "An' if some'm happen to me." Looking at him, like he better protect her. "You be strung by a rope!"

Stepping back from her. Like she's a snake. "Shut…up." He stutters, "Na…no one's g-getting hung." Shaking his head. "No one's getting hurt. I give you water, you know that. You c'n tell um!"

"We got'a think of Brutha."

"Brutha?"

"What he gon' do? With you locked up. Who

gonna help him den." She waits for Hector to untwist that in his mind. "But…" That's when she sees a chance as his head slowly turns back from that door. "If'n you free me. I'll tell the authorities not to lock you up."

He stares at her a moment. Then like a wet dog shakes his head, trying to get all her words out of his ears. "Cain't." He backs further away from her. His foot hits the wall. "Brutha, he say, *watch her.*"

Taking another sip of water, she takes a new tact. *Arguing is thirsty work.* "You be doing Brutha a favor, Hector." He still looks at her like a snake about to strike, but Beneda's smile remains. "He don't want to go to jail. You don't want that, neither."

He shakes his head. "No, ma'am."

She hears M'Deah, many years back, *folk love t'talk 'bout theyselves.* "Hector. What parts of the country you been to?"

Now, his eyes get big, she sees he's thinking, *this seem easy. Not about doing something he shouldn't*. "I been t' Georgia and all through the Carolinas." Looking to the door again. "Brutha says we gots to keep moving."

"Really? I ain't been to so many places." She looks down to the rope on her left ankle. "You think I ever gonna see those places?"

Hector takes one step forward, gulping. But, still not getting too close. "Sure, Miss Beneda. Mista' Cootuh, he say we let'n you go."

Strike now. "Well if'n he say to let me go…You *can* let me go. Now…"

That big head shakes again. "No. I's got a wait for Brutha."

Beneda lets out a dramatic sigh. "Okay. But,

Brutha and Mista' Cootuh be disappointed. In you."

Hector opens his mouth, but turns at a scratching at the door. "That you Brutha?"

Brutha walks in. Cootuh behind him. He holds a cloth out to Hector, keeps another for himself. "Here, cornbread."

Cootuh adds, "And butter."

Dropping his club, Hector grabs the covered food and stuffs his mouth full.

"Miss Beneda. Would you like some'a this here cornbread?" By the light of the oil lamp, Cootuh steps in front of Beneda, and she reads something there in those shifting eyes of his.

She controls her near-grimace. *Be friendly.* But, she won't break bread with these fools. "No." Genteel, through gritted teeth, she adds, "I do thank you, all the same. Hector was kind enough to offer me water already."

"The town's in uproar. You must be more important than you thought." He looks at his men, both shoveling in that cornbread, now that there's more to go around. "There be search parties in the woods. We almost got caught." Brutha hitches up his overalls, and stops just short of spitting at that news. "We'll wait till midnight. To free you. Should be quieter then. Nobody wants any trouble here. You see?"

She stares in Cootuh's face, and sweetly announces, "They will never stop looking for you."

10 Rescue - Heart

Aza whines and paws at the bundle of clothes. Lakisha spots a red ribbon stretched across the alleyway, keeping folks from trampling the crime's scene. No-see-ums buzz about her head. Cold night air bites her nose. Torches and lanterns held by several men and women seem to draw the small gnats. And the lights add to the glint of moon; excited voices rise in the night. The library woman, Zenobia points to the bundle that Aza is worrying his noses through.

"The woman there provided those clothes from Miss Beneda."

A big woman waves her lantern at the scout. "We searched dem woods to the north. Ain't seen nothin' yet."

Asante points into the alley protected by the ribbon. "Zenobia. How many people have been in this alley tonight?"

Zenobia rubs the big bruise on the side of her head. "Lots after the attack. Looking. Some just curious." Waving in the direction of the library. "Once Librarian Oliver got your message, we did our best."

"Shooed people out." The big girl moves closer to Aza, peering down at him. "Can your dog really find Beneda?"

Glancing at the girl before bending to examine

the disturbed dirt in the alley, then murmurs. “Yes. Aza can follow anyone.” Turning to Zenobia, he dismisses the question and demands, “Tell me again.”

Zenobia steps up to the ribboned-off alley, and points. “We walked east toward the library. They came from the alley.” She swings her hand at her head. “One hit me. The other lifted her up. They headed back down the alley. I fell. Once we got back to the Library and our exchange of messages, I came back to Marquetta; for the girl’s clothes as you asked.”

Turning back to the big girl, the scout now has questions for her, “You went through the alley. Where does it go, Marquetta?”

Nodding, she points down the darkened way. “De alley end at the small stream behin’ town.”

He examines Marquetta’s face in the flicking light, then decides. “Okay. We’ll go now. Who is coming?”

Marquetta holds her lantern up and shakes the club in her fist. “Ima comin’.” Shaking that club at an older man, she adds, “Turner be comin’ too.” The thin, but tough looking man, carrying a long kitchen knife, just grunts his assent.

“Okay, everybody else stay back.” Placing a hand on Lakisha’s shoulder, Asante offers a quieter instruction, “Stay close to Aza. Carry the bundle. Case he needs another sniff. If he flushes men out, and he might, stay back. Let Aza and us handle them.”

Nodding, rubbing sleep from her eyes Lakisha steps over, and scoops up the bundle. Ready for what may come next.

Near an hour later Lakisha's feet hurt. It's hard to keep Aza in sight. The pup is such a good tracker. The moon's glow partly blocked by the trees has turned Aza into a fast moving shadow. Marquetta's lantern just a pale glob. Asante walks silently before Lakisha, head swiveling. Turner tramps noisily with Marquetta, behind. The ground's flat, but woody.

Why the search parties found nothing? Lakisha thinks as she observes the scout freezing up ahead. *Stay with Aza,* she remembers. Continuing to step carefully, she glances back, her bundle of Beneda's clothes gripped tight to her chest.

Turner pauses next to Asante, his knife shining in the moonlight. Suddenly the two men launch themselves to the left. Looking that way, Lakisha thinks she sees someone moving. Marquetta, behind her, stops a moment, *who to follow must be in her mind*. There are shouts, from both Turner and the scout. Lakisha watches Marquetta as she looks to the men, then at back at Aza.

Then Lakisha sees she's decided, Marquetta starts up again after the guide. Turning back, Lakisha's glance follows the dog's tail, disappearing around a bush. Aza's focus only on what scents he's been given to track, not who may be following him.

Listening in the dimness, the girls track Aza by his soft padding up ahead. Suddenly, Lakisha steps onto a path. Up a ways, Aza sniffs at something. Peering down the dim flat way, Lakisha sees a clearing, *Has Aza found something?* With a small shack a good couple of meters to the left. She stops. Marquetta bumps into her from the darkness behind.

Silently, Lakisha points to it. Aza continues padding toward the shack. "What we do?" she whispers

Marquetta raises her club and hisses like some villain in a minstrel show. A hiss that carries, “Save Benetta!”

They creep slowly into that clearing. Aza crouches in front of the door, tail high, and slowly sweeping back and forth. Lakisha doesn’t know quite what to do.

Stopping close behind Aza, his tail brushes their toes.

With a loud thud, the door opens. First one big man steps out, then a second. Both have clubs, that second one holds a lamp. Past his body, Lakisha sees a chair dimly in the room. *Beneda.*

Nobody moves. Aza rises slightly, still crouched, but higher. A deep growl vibrates his body. Marquetta takes a step forward, her club raised.

“Stop, you.” Marquetta’s voice sounds a mite squeaky. But her stance seem to mean business.

The big man in front nods to the other. “Scat!” Then he breaks into a run toward the woods. In a second the other man joins him, bolting off the rickety porch.

~~~

The girls are left standing outside the shack. Lakisha holds her breath till a sound comes from the darkness inside. A squeak and a shuffle of something heavy. Then comes cursing like she’s only heard from Stick going after one of the littl’uns.

Marquetta swings the lantern to each side, examining the shadows and Beneda’s face appears at the doorway. Lakisha stares, then sputters, “Aza! Go find Asante! Bring ’im here.”
~~~

The dog lopes off back down the path.

Shaking, a little, Beneda seems okay. They work at comforting, rubbing her wrists and feeling her brow; though she seems to need precious little of that. And the three remain in the dark yard, with only Marquetta's lantern against the night. Waiting for the scout.

Can't 'magine what it's like, held by strange men.

Asante strides into the clearing, Aza at his heel. Behind them Turner follows.

"Whoever it is got away," the scout announces.

Beneda shakes her head. "That was probably Cootuh." Biting her lip. Then spitting out, "He slipped off early. Making sure he'd avoid capture, no doubt."

Appraising her from top to bottom, Asante then inquires, "Are you all right?"

"Yes." Smiling at him, her hand rubbing dirt from her face, she adds, "They didn't hurt me."

Looking down at Aza, he says, "I was very worried."

Lakisha notices Beneda's mouth turning up a tiny bit. She decides to help with this.

"Yeah, Miss. We been riding all night. To get here." Then she points to the scout. "An' he got somethin' for you."

First giving Lakisha a sharp glance, his smile quickly turns. Then a cough. "Yes," as his eyes move back to Beneda, he straightens his vest, explaining, "I have copies of the land deeds."

Marquetta grabs Beneda's shoulders. "Fer real?"

Nodding, he points back to the path past Turner, who waits with the lantern Marquetta's shoved into his keeping. The scout advises, "Let's get back to town."

The three farmers walk together, Turner holding Marquetta's lantern high. Lakisha, the scout, and Aza follow.

Up ahead, Turner addresses Beneda, voices carrying back to the rear guard. "I'll ride back first thing in the morning. Tell all dem the news."

"Thank you." Beneda nods. "Marquetta, Bessie and I will walk back later in the day…"

Asante waves at Lakisha in the dimness, he lowers his tone, for her ears only. "Lakisha. Best you and Aza stay with Beneda tonight."

"Don't worry. We keep her safe."

~~~

In the corner of Beneda's room, Lakisha's eyes bounce to each person as they speak. She sits with Aza, her thin arms around his warm neck. Her eyes feel heavy, but she can't stop listening, A clock strikes two long *bongs*.

The girl focuses on Marquetta's hands, rubbing together, *like she washin'*. Her voice too loud for the time of night. Turner and Miss Bessie wince and pat with dey hands to shush her. "Beneda. You *knows* you gots't ask dat scout t' come wit' us."

"Yes. I'll ask the scout to come to the farms." Lakisha thinks, *She speakin' to calm her friend, anything to keep the heifer quiet.* "No one believe me otherwise."

Turner's head shakes. "Miss Beneda. Dat ain't it. People believe whatever you tell."

Lakisha notices how the other woman, Miss Bessie, be nodding, *tired out poor thing*, but adds all the same, "That right. Girl, all folks trust you. Now."
~~~

The man puts his hand on the doorknob. “Ima goin’. One drink in de bar, then bed.” Waving the kitchen knife he sill ain’t let ago of, he apologizes to these ladies, “Got’s to return this. I’ma lookin’ forward to gettin’ home to my son.”

Bessie steps over Lakisha to him and kisses his cheek. Turner’s son manages the Brown farm. Lakisha’s mouth mimics the drop she sees on the other girls’ as Bessie hugs Turner before he leaves. Closing the door, all the girls stare at Bessie.

Marquetta steps over and grabs the older woman’s hand. “Bessie?”

But Bessie, she pull her hand back. “Non’ you need be worrit ‘bout. I’ma going. See you in da morning.” She too rushes out the door.

Beneda and Marquetta look at each other and giggle softly behind they hands.

Marquetta points. “May be old. But, dey still alive.”

Snickering Beneda adds, “Sleepy. I need to clean up. And sleep.”

“You gots to get your beauty rest. For *him.*” Marquetta nods. Slowly.

Shaking her head, but all Beneda gives in return is, “Get on to bed, Marquetta.”

But Marquetta, she don’t let it go. Not at all, once again that voice fills Beneda’s room, “After all, he say, he *worrit* ‘bout you. Why, he left his dog. An Lakisha!” She waves to act the fool, calling, “Ain’t that right, Lakisha?”

Lakisha nods, sleepily. Still hearing those two clock *bongs*.

Pushing her friend toward the door, Beneda just scolds, “Shut up. Go to bed.”

Marquetta lets herself be shoved to the door. Opening it, she parts with, “Jus’ make sure you look good, tomorra. For *Assaantee.*”

Shaking her head, Beneda closes the door behind her. Turning to Lakisha. “You okay, there on the boys’ blankets?”

“Yes’sum…” Lakisha’s eyes are already closed. She hugs the warm pup to her and smiles.

11 Farmer's Life - Heart

When morning's come, Lakisha, in the Library's dining room, places a warm bowl in front of the scout. Informing him proudly about her kitchen work. "Cook has me helpin'. Choppin' and fixin' fruits."

Asante sets to, spooning honey onto his porridge. "That's great you got something to do."

Lakisha wipes her hands on the borrowed apron, as hard as it was rising this morning, she's so glad she did. "I'ma write mama. Tell her I'm helpin' here." The Librarian enters the dining room. "Some porridge, Librarian, sir?" she asks with a bow.

Smiling and shaking his head, Librarian Oliver now has a smile for the scout's little guide. "No, thank you, my dear." Stopping beside the scout, he asks, "You speak to the farmers yet, this morning?"

Nodding, Asante lowers the spoon. "Yes."

"I agree you should take these to the farmers." He blusters, places papers on the table at the scout's elbow. "See that each farm gets them handed over in person." Librarian Oliver points to the stack. "Zenobia organized copies made of them. So, you'll hand these over."

Asante nods thoughtfully. Lakisha notices he hesitates before speaking. "How do you think Cootuh knew about the farmer's movements?"

"I will question my staff again, someone may know." The Librarian's eyes scan the scout's face. "Surely you don't suspect anyone here?"

"I don't know who to suspect." Shaking his head, Asante looks down at his bowl. And simply states, "Someone is telling the thugs where to be."

"Please, my good sir. Convince the farmers the library had nothing to do with these tragic events."

With that side to side waggle of his head, Asante responds, "I shall try."

A grimace crossing his face, the Librarian takes the assurance and walks out.

"Lakisha." The scout turns to her, now. "You may stay and help Cook, or come with me to the farms. Which do you prefer?"

Staring at him with joy, she tries thinking about this. "Really?"

"Miss Beneda says she hopes you'll visit. So she can thank you properly." He smiles wide. "For saving her life." Aza copies with a dog smile all his own.

Pointing, she smiles and shakes her head. "Aza did it."

Nodding, the scout reaches down and pats his pup's head. "That's why he's coming to the farms, too."

~~~

On the road, Lakisha and Aza lead the group. Beneda walks next with Asante. Further back come Miss Bessie and Marquetta. Lakisha's glad they've almost arrived. It's been a long walk from Bluffton. Behind her she hears, Beneda, "It's 'round the next bend that our Gullah farmlands start." There's a pause, and only footsteps sound. "You were—
~~~

wonderful—to come looking for me." Lakisha listens to Beneda praising the scout, her tone seems to be hiding nerves.

Why cain't folks jus talk to each other?

The scout, he says, "You are important—" Lakisha hangs on this pause. "—To the farmers." *Sheesh.*

"We farmers don't know how to fight," Beneda's words hiding maybe disappointment, "We have a need for skills like yours."

Pausing again, a moment passes before he talks. "I hope you don't have to fight. Like I have." Lakisha doesn't know what he means, but it's not her business, let 'em not talk like they been doin'.

Beneda, she disagrees, "But everyone respects library scouts." Then she get her turn to do some pauses. "You are admired by everyone."

Lakisha picks up a stick, makes her own nonsense noise with it. Under that sound, Asante responds with a low voice, "It's only important to be admired by the right ones."

So quietly Lakisha can barely hear what comes from Beneda, next, "I admire you."

Just sounds of breathing. *I ain't gonna look back.* "And, you are important to me. I had to help you." Lakisha steps softly beside Aza. Not wanting to let the two think about her listening.

"I was worried you wouldn't help," Beneda raises her voice. Just a little. "After what Librarian Oliver did."

Lakisha next hears a noise she didn't expect from the scout, and wonders what would make him do that. Even Aza looks back at Asante. "What did the Librarian do?" Asante asks. Lakisha, doesn't want to turn, *mebbe their hands are close, but not quite touchin'*. She don't need to see that. Lakisha thinks how this might affect her work in the kitchen.

Now Beneda takes a deep breath. "He wrote a letter. It said we farmers should sell our land."

"Well." He exhales loudly. "He made a wrong decision. I will talk to him about—"

Beneda interrupts, "—I don't want to cause trouble."

"Libraries exist to serve the community." Raising his voice, even Marquetta and Bessie stop they talkin', he reminds, "They lead and serve the people. They are not working to help only the rich."

Lakisha hears a slap against cloth, *theys getting closer now, I keep my eyes front fo' sure*. "You brought the solution to our problems. I'm not worried about the Librarian."

"Yes," Asante agrees. "But, are the ones who want the land convinced?"

"It's nearly the end of spring." Lakisha thinks Beneda's tone means she wants to ask for something. "The harvest's coming soon. We can't worry about those bad ones."

It's quiet back there for a minute. Risking a look, Lakisha sees the two *are* walking close together. A meter back, the other women stare.

"Beneda. I want to protect you." Asante only sees Beneda, not Lakisha.

But, Beneda, she does. "Lakisha. Go ask Marquetta, and Bessie, dey comin' to my place?"

Darn. dis was jus get'n interestin'. "Yas'um" Glancing down, she pats at the pup's head. "See you in a minute, Aza."

Dropping back to the others, Lakisha sees their

eagerness for gabbing.

Grabbing her arm, Marquetta demands. "Spill it, Girl."

She ignores what Marquetta wants. "Miss Beneda want t'know. You comin't her place?"

The big girl gives her arm a rough little shake. "Dat not what I want to know."

The other, Bessie, helps Lakisha, a smile and a touch to her head, she say, "I'ma stop at the Brown place."

That gets Marquetta's attention. She lets loose. "Where Turner be?"

Bessie ignores that. "'Quetta. Where you goin'?"

Shaking her head, Marquetta glances between Bessie, Lakisha and the couple ahead. "Y'all vex me!" Back to Lakisha. "I'ma goin' home. Now. Tell Beneda *dat*! An tell her, invite me ta de wedding." She sets the girl running.

Hurrying back to the couple, Lakisha blurts as she runs past, "Miss Bessie goin' a Brown place! Miss Marquetta goin' home!"

~~~

The nine-year-old, Caleb came up, running, whooping at them as they passed Old Lady Harris's place. This here Caleb tugs at Lakisha's arm. She holds him back. Keeping him from bothering Aza. Him, he say, "I'ma visit ma frien' Jolan!" And he tagged along with their group.

At their final stop on this long journey, Lakisha finally has a moment to look up in wonder at the big house. She kneels, telling the pup, "It's huge, and fine."

"Hello, Missus Washington," Asante bows to the
~~~

woman standing out front. Beneda's mother. "I'm pleased to meet you."

"Welcome to our farm, Scout Asante." She admires his vest. "My daughter has written of you." No one much looks at Lakisha, nor her dusty bare feet. Missus Washington adds, "Turner speaks highly of you. Thank you. For everything." Lakisha watches Beneda frown and rub her sandal in the dirt.

Caleb pipes up. "De librarian has de land papers!"

The older woman looks at the little one. "Caleb. Go find Jolan." At his tug, Lakisha lets his hand go. Aza be safe now. With a shake of her head, Beneda's Mama calls after the boy, "Stay out of trouble."

"Mister Asante." Gazing up at his face. Missus Washington waves at the house. "Please come in. Get on out of the sun."

"Thank you."

Following the others up onto the wide porch, Lakisha points at Aza. "Stay here."

Beneda and the scout wipe their sandals on the rug at the door, before the well-polished space of the large front room. Lakisha does the same with her bare feet.

"This farm survives on corn and vegetables," Missus Washington's explains over her shoulder. Back erect, voice calm, "We ship to the nearby towns."

"I've been impressed," Asante gives praise, "how your neighbors have been working together."

"Scout Asante." The woman reaches for his arm. "Join me in the study." Then to her daughter, "Beneda, get us some lemon water and fruit. And, little one?"

"Lakisha," she says with a dip.

"Lakisha, you go on, help."

"Yas'um." She follows Beneda, her bare feet pat-patting down the hall. In the kitchen, she asks, "I'll take some water to Aza, Miss?"

Beneda nods, pointing to a bowl on the counter, then takes up a knife for fruit.

Setting the bowl on the porch, Lakisha stands for a moment, hearing Aza lap water, watching the sunset cast stains of pink and maroon that melt into violet shadows on fields of corn. She hears a soft guitar, strumming, from a shack, and sees Caleb chasing a boy who must be Jolan away from the beehives, against the far side of the yard.

Returning to the kitchen, she picks up bowls of cut fruit that Beneda points her knife at. Then, joins her going back through the spotless hallways to the study.

"…my daughter—" Missus Washington stops as the pair enters.

With a nod, Beneda directs Lakisha to set the fruit on the largest table. She adds a gourd with lemon water and cups on the tray she carries, no one speaks of the smile gracing her face.

"Help yourself," Beneda points to the spread. Lakisha watches her fine hand pouring from the gourd and Beneda handing that first cup to the scout.

As Lakisha takes up a slice of peach, cutting her eyes, to study each person in turn. Settling on the mama's face, she sees the gray at the temples and crow's feet at the corners of those dark eyes.

"Scout Asante." The woman addresses him, *Oh*

yes, this woman runs this house. "I picked out a room for you. Soon's Turner told us how you saved my daughter."

Outside, Aza barks in excited yips, those boys must be close. The scout, he only says, "Beneda tells us they were going to free her without hurting her."

"Can't trust those criminals."

The scout nods. "I'm happy that Aza, Marquetta, and Lakisha found your daughter."

Missus Washington gestures her daughter over. "Beneda. Scout Asante tells me he ain't married."

Beneda's choking noise rings loud in the study. Lakisha sees her throat bob, trying to swallow a bit of peach. "Maa-ma! …Mister Asante has the property deeds." Reminds Lakisha of Caleb's shout a few minutes ago, high and excited.

The scout he nods. Then sets his bag on a chair. After a moment searching through the papers, he hands one to Missus Washington.

The mother looks intently at the one page, her daughter forgotten. Finally, she turns it over, examining both sides, touching the paper as if it were a loved one. "Ain't no library seal on dis paper."

Asante gives her a slight bow and a nod. "It's a copy. The original's in Beaufort. Locked up."

After a moment, she nods. "Well then. Thank you for this."

Asante pats the bag. "I need to get these others to all the farmers."

Rubbing her hands on her dress. "Good excuse. We always have a harvest party. A week early is fine. I'll bring all the farmers here. Tomorrow night," Missus Washington orders.

12 Bossman - Trickster

The maid, Faith, leads Cootuh into the Hardeeville dining room. He’s faced with just the three, clustered at one end of the long table. Buckra, his daughter, and Malcolm.

Buckra glances up from his plate. All but bellows, “Finally! Cootuh. We expected you hours ago.” Waving to a place beside Malcolm. “Join us? We mostly finished. But, cook sure has leftovers.”

Shaking his head, Cootuh pats at his pants, tugs at his collar. “No. Thank you sir. I gots to get cleaned up.”

Malcolm only casts a foul expression his way. Octavia sips at her red wine in its fine crystal. One door swings open, revealing Jeremiah, who carries in a tray with deserts, wearing ill-fitting livery. Looking no better than Cootuh at the moment.

Pointing to the new servant, the boss brags. “Our newest man in service. Malcolm, thought it won’t work. But, I told him, *anyone* can succeed. Just have to dress them up right.”

Cootuh studies Jeremiah’s awkward serving, how he fumbles setting down the small plate. How he looks uncomfortable and unhappy.

Now for the bad news, “Sir, we had a setback with the farmers.”

Malcolm *harumphs*. “We?”

Cootuh waits. It's for the boss to respond. Finally, Jeremiah having backed away, Buckra glances down at the plate and nods. "Yes?"

"The farmers are well organized and determined."

The boss looks to Malcolm. "You assured me they weren't."

Malcolm's fist tightens on his folk, he tenses, with an embarrassed look darkening his cheeks. "But. They weren't. A week ago."

When the boss' look darts back to him, Cootuh risks some explaining, "There're a few key people. They're giving backbone and purpose to the others."

Malcolm sets his fork down. Loud on the china. "I'll go!"

But Buckra holds up his hand. "Perhaps a gentler touch will work." Then he turns his stern gaze to his daughter. "Maybe you can pay a visit, Octavia? Try a little persuasion?"

Her glance tracks over to her father. Painted lips tilt up in a faint smile.

~~~

With Mister Buckra out of the room. Malcolm stares intently, Cootuh bowels go a bit wammy, hearing, "Cootuh, You need to make me look good in front of the boss. Hear?"

Got him. He's desperate, thinks Cootuh. He'll gentle down this fool the best he can, using his words as whitewash, "Has he said something to you—Boss?"

Jeremiah scoots around them, eyes down, clearing the table. Octavia sips from her wine glass. As if their exchange is mere chatter from the help.
~~~

"He doesn't understand our challenge." Malcolm stretches in his dinner jacket. Face going that dark again. "We need to convince these farmers, without getting caught breaking the law, or upsetting the libraries."

Sitting back, Octavia reaches into her reticule, her long fingers hold up a small mirror to check her face. Jeremiah's tray clatters as he slips out carefully. Cootuh sees he don't want to even turn his back on the room.

Cootuh tries reassuring, offering a soft, "We'll know if there's a problem with the libraries."

"Yes, your contact." Malcolm removes his jacket, *He wouldn't if the big boss was still sittin' there*. "How far do you trust them?"

"Not far." Cootuh shakes his head, *no need to take that line of thought farther, just yet*. "They're getting nervous. We all thought, this was going to go quickly."

Turning to Octavia, Malcolm adds, "We need to stay on good terms with them." *Like she don't already know.*

Setting down her mirror, she gives a cat's smile. "I will see what I can do about our relations with those *book* folks." This to Malcolm, Cootuh only gets ignored.

Nodding, Cootuh takes that. *Okay Miss*. But he suggests anyway, "When we get to Beaufort, we can see how to separate the farmers and the librarians."

Malcolm rises to his feet. "Have a good trip." Pausing, all but dismissing any more Cootuh might have to say. "'member, you protect Mister Buckra's family name."

~~~
~~~

Malcolm's left the dining room. Cootuh's stayed.

He watches Jeremiah polishing the furniture, and Octavia walking around the table. She stops and stares up before her, at a painting on the wall. A portrait of a plain woman, but vividly painted.

Without turning, speaking more to the air than the two still in the room, Octavia asks, "What do you think of that? Do you know about pictures?"

Cootuh cuts her a look, "What is there to know?"

She frowns in Jeremiah's direction, touches a light hand to her neck. "To know? Everything that defines us and our lives." Cootuh thinks how different she is from the farmer girl he had imprisoned. *Different worlds*.

Pointing up, she commands, "Look closely. What do you see?"

"Your great-grandmother?" Cootuh remembers.

"You're not looking properly." Now she turns and perhaps she sees him. "Do you know what my father used to do with me when I was little? I'd be forced get up on the buffet table. 'To see it properly', he said."

"Seriously?" Just seems like a family portrait to him.

"Stand here." She gestures him closer. "See now? Isn't she beautiful?"

"Well, no. But, she looks … kind of like *him*." Shaking his head in the direction of the door.

"So, you see it. He looks like her. Now when my picture is up there, my grandson will look like me." Octavia smiles. That scary feline smile. "I can die happy."

"I guess. You are your father's daughter."

She waves at the large window. “This is our world. As far as the eye can see. Someday, it will be all mine.”

Cootuh touches his hand to his forehead, gives a dip she probably feels she deserves, and says, “I ought to get to work on our trip.” Changing topic. “Can I use Jeremiah?”

Octavia sniffs, “Take him.”

Nodding, he slides over to Jeremiah, low out of her hearing, he ask, “How you doing?”

“I needs a drink.” His yellowed eyes say, *that ain’t no lie.*

Cootuh holds out a hand, low just for the boy to see. “Hold on. I’ma get you out of here.”

“You can?” A brief smile chases a frown across Jeremiah face.

“You’re going on a trip with us.” The smile again. “Organize three riding horses for us. One pack horse.”

Jeremiah shoves the little polish tin and his rag into his pocket, going toward the door with a new posture and bounce. Malcolm, walking in the door, stares at the boy in passing.

With one glance back, Malcolm holds a paper to Cootuh. “Here is the claim from Liberia.” As Cootuh takes it, Malcolm warns, “Might’n not stand up in court. But, maybe you can scare someone with it.”

Octavia steps toward the door. “I’m going to get ready. How much time do I have?”

Cootuh gestures down at his dirty clothes. “Give me two hours. I’m going to the kitchen. Pack up some food for our trip.”

As she leaves, Malcolm gives him a funny look. “This life seems to suit you?”

Cootuh puts on a silly grin. “Why, not?” Pointing to the door, vacant after Octavia’s passing. “Seeing the world.” He nods to the painting, “With a pretty woman.”

Malcolm speaks through gritted teeth. “See that you don’t lose that paper…or Mister Buckra’s daughter.”

We best both make sure Mister Buckra stay alive.

13 Farmer Party - Soul

Carrying a water-jug in each hand, Jolan wishes he could play with Caleb. But, Missus Washington, she say, “No. Not ’til the party starts!” It should be soon now. *Hours of wagons arriv’in*. Setting the jugs down on one of the rows of tables in the flat field next to the big house, shooin’ the bees from the cold lemonade.

Jolan sets his hands on his hips, counting jugs and the places that need ‘em. Scanning round to see what he’s suppos’t do next. Seeing Beneda waving at him, he scampers toward her. “Yas’um, Miss Beneda?” Jolan stares at the huge mound of corn on a sheet in front of Pete there on a bench.

“Set yourself. We shuck’n corn.” Beneda points to Pete, already sitting.

Dragging himself to the bench’s other end, Jolan plops hisself down, complains, “This’ll take hours.”

Beneda, she only reminds the boys, “M’Deah said, ‘sooner started, sooner done’.”

With a frown, Jolan sets to grab a cob. He thinks, *when I gets big I’ma run away to where der ain’t never be a corn cob again*. Beneda carries a bucket over and sets it up between the two.

Pete don’t look at Beneda, asking while shucking. “Miss Bessie, she say you be spendin’ a lot of time with the library scout there in town. That true?"

"I beg your pardon?" Beneda stops with a cob in her hands, the husk and tassels grasped and ready to pull. "What you say'n?"

Pete stops, now only Jolan works. "She say, she jus' saw yous," he ducks and picks up a new ear, "always with him. Jus' wonder'd."

Turning away, Beneda pulls at the tassels, straight down in one firm tug. "*Him.*" Another tug. "Asante is his name." Husks into the bucket, corn tossed onto the clean sheet. "*He* is a guest on my farm."

Seeing Beneda pick another cob, hearing her tone, he's startled back to work himself, yet Pete keeps on it, "I'm just wondering." Jolan can't stop listen'n to their talking. Though Beneda's just about clammed up now. Pete continues the chatter, Beneda ignores it and Jolan, he just keeps his shoulders hunched. "What's he to you?"

She cuts her eyes to Pete for a moment. "Have you asked that question of everyone?"

Stuttering, Pete shucks and talks, "B…But. I don't care about them."

"Thanks for your concern." Her voice sounds icy to Jolan. She's still sitting more facing him, away from Pete. "No," she says to the air between them. "You need not concern yourself on that score."

Jolan watches the something that flickers across Pete's face. Hearing her then add, "at least I don't think so…"

~~~

Now at the crowded table Jolan gets squeezed between Beneda and Missus Washington. He spies
~~~

Caleb at another table with Mister Turner and Miss Bessie, cutting peaches. His friend is trying to juggle some. Pete sits with his grandma. Two chairs away. Jolan's counting faces. Nothin' else to do.

Pounding the table with her hand, Missus Washington speaks up. "We all here about the land papers." She holds hers high overhead then she points to the scout.

Pulling out papers from his bag, Asante hands them over to Beneda. Standing, she reads the first one and hands it to Mister Turner's son. Then the next one goes to Old Lady Harris. Beneda hands the next to Jolan, he scoots from his chair and runs it to the end of the long table, Missus Hogg gives him a smile for hers. Soon, they're all handed out and everyone's set down again, reaching for the corn and every other fixin's in hand's reach.

Jolan breaks a piece of bread, and slips his hand down to his lap, he hands it to the pup, Aza, set back on his haunches, keeping an eye on the scout. The dog looks to Asante. At his nod, Aza reaches out and eases the morsel from Jolan's fingertips.

"Well, our problems are over then?" the Turner boy asks. "We have proof we own our farms?"

Waving her paper, Old Lady Harris shakes her head. "Ain't no seal on dis here paper."

Beneda glances to the scout, then speaks to the gathering, "These are copies Scout Asante has brought us." Nodding to him. "The originals bide locked in Beaufort."

Shaking her head again, Old Lady stares at the scout. "The originals we need."

Looking directly at Old Lady, "Official documents have already disappeared from the

Bluffton Library," he explains to her alone, after a moment he glances around the long tables. "It'd be a risk bringing those only copies. You don't want that to happen again."

Young Turner speaks up. "Are you saying the library can't protect official documents?"

Looking toward Beneda, the scout answers, "The library in Bluffton has limited resources."

With a cackling laugh Old Lady slams the paper down. "What he mean, dey cain't be trusted."

~~~

Hours later, the party is still loud and busy, Jolan feels like he's drunk his weight in lemonade. Like Caleb next to him, snoring on a pile of burlap, Jolan feels the need to nap. He thinks of the long day of hauling, peeling, and sitting, why he's so sleepy. He leans on the dog, who's sat by his side. Beneda and the scout set on a near bench.

"Pete is going to Beaufort to get the documents."

"Not a good idea." Their voices come to the boy, who struggles a bit less each second.

"I agree with you. I said so. The others insisted."

Jolan leans back against Calab. Staring at the lights of the party through dropping eyelids. He spies those near him. His eyes fighting sleep.

"I will try to shore up security at the library." The scout touches Beneda's knee. "I worry about your safety and future."

"Will you go back home." Eyes closed now, near surrender, Jolan hears her gulp. "After this is over."

The scout does not speak for a moment. "I don't know where home is. Anymore."

Jolan imagines lamplight flickering in Beneda's
~~~

eyes. “You could think about making a home here. In Bluffton, perhaps?”

Turning, Jolan shifts, he opens his eyes to see Pete striding up. Scout Asante opens his mouth. Jolan notices Beneda sitting up straighter, pulling her arms in tight.

“Ah, Beneda. And, Asante.” Pete steps close. “Lookin’ for you.” He offers a small bow. “It’s getting late.”

Her eyes sleepy, Beneda focuses on Pete. “You have my permission to retire, Pete.”

Frowning and shaking his head. “You should go inside. Your mother has gone to bed.” *Why Pete talkin’ so proper?*

“Thank you. I’m not tired. I’ll stay here.” She brushes her hair away from her forehead, and reaches over and pats the scout’s leg. “Here with Asante.”

Pete’s frown turns fiercer. “I’m leaving first thing.” Jolan sees how those eyes dwell on the two sitting close. Then Pete’s looking at the two boys huddled together. “I’m taking Caleb. Jolan, you want to come wit us?”

Nodding, Jolan looks to Beneda. For her nod. “Yes, please, Mister Pete.”

Reaching down Pete scoops up Caleb, gives a curt nod for Jolan to come too.

“When I get back. The problems will be solved.” Glancing back. “Then, Mister Asante can return to Africa.”

14 Seduction - Soul

On the second day, all Jolan has on his mind is how tired he is of this long barefoot walk to Beaufort.

"I wish Caleb could'a come wit us."

Pete looks down at the smaller boy. "He sick."

"He et too much at the party," Jolan complains. "That girl, Lakisha, says they rode a carriage into Beaufort. To da library. Why didn't we ride?"

Pete reminds him. "Lakisha, she traveling with the scout." Both boys so glad now, that the town's here. No more walkin' today. Pete says more to hisself than to Jolan, "Mos' times, library staff, dey ride for free."

Jolan thinks, *Pete, he sure don't like scouts*. They're jostled on the busy path. In town now. So many things to see.

"'cuse me, sir," Pete asks a well-dressed man. "Where be the library?"

Pausing, the man points, "Two or three blocks north." He takes in their dusty feet, and the sweat on Jolan's shirt collar, and answers, "It's on Scott Street. I think three eleven Scott."

"Let's go, Jolan." Jolan's dragging, *more to go?* He straightens though, when he reckons Pete's examining him. No one stares at a shadow for no good reason. "We soon can sit somewheres."

After three long blocks, Jolan finally sees a brick building, both boys forget these last blocks and the hours behind them, Jolan shouts, “There!”

With his smaller stride, Jolan drags his heels up the brick steps. The light blinds him, coming back from the big window beside the door.

Inside, blinking, he spies a man behind a desk, who’s lifted his eyes to the pair. “Greetings to the Beaufort Library.”

“H…Hello.” Pete stutters, his hands in front of him holding an invisible cap in his shaking hands. “I’m, I’ma come for the L…Librarian.”

“Of course.” Smiling big, he spreads his hands, asking, “May I tell her your business?”

“We from the Farms. On Daufuskie Island.”

“Ah, yes.” The young man rises. “Come, shall I have you wait in a meeting room?”

Jolan stares up at the high ceilings and windows. Nods *yes*, at this question. Books are everywhere. In a smaller room the smiling library man leaves them to sit at one of the shiniest tables he’s ever seen.

Sitting accomplished, next Jolan asks, “When we gonna eat, Pete?”

“Soon’s we leave.” Pete’s voice is the church voice his gramma, Old Lady Harris, is always pinching his arm to get him to use. *Respectful*. “We gots to book a room. And I gots one more thing to do.”

“Aw, Pete. We’s hungry. An’ tired.”

“I know. Just wait.”

Jolan sits, but Pete, he stands straighter as a fancy dressed woman comes in. The gray in her hair makes her eyes seem wise.

“Welcome, young men.” Her hand goes out, as

she asks Pete, "You are?"

"Ma'am. Pete Harris." And his hands do that cap thing again. She turns her eyes to the shiny table, and Jolan slumping there. Not kickin' his feet at all. "This is Jolan," Pete tells her, and fumbling in his jacket, he finds the paper. "This he—*Here is* a letter from my grandmother. Asking for the land deed originals. It's signed by all ten farm owners." Jolan's heard him mumble these words for the last thirty miles of their trip.

"Yes." She nods, looking sad. "We received a pigeon, warning us that you were coming." Shaking her head, she examines the paper, then tucks it into a fold of her robe. "We have not decided whether to agree to this or not."

Jolan notices Pete is putting on a hangdog look. "But, Ma'am…"

With a raised hand, the Librarian cuts him off. *A school teacher stopping a wrong answer*, Jolan thinks.

"I'm going to consult with Bluffton. By pigeon." Her faces lights with a small smile as Pete's shoulders lower an inch. "Maybe, even other libraries. You will have an answer tomorrow."

Nothing more to say. Bowing, Pete thanks her, "Ma'am."

First touching her robe where the paper's now tucked away, then her hand shoos them away, lightly, that smile till there. "Go now. Come back after noon, boys. Tomorrow."

Reaching the door, Jolan bleats, "Hungry."

That helps. Though Pete gives a shove. The Librarian stops them, "Forgive me, boys, allow me to tell the kitchen that you should get a slice of buttered bread and an apple to take before you go."

"Old Lady Harris told me 'bouta place t' spend the night." Pete moves quickly now that they're back on the street. "Then, jus' one more task."

Jolan *humphs*. He gnaws at the last of his apple core. And tries keeping up, thirty kilometers and no end in sight.

After walking a few more blocks, Pete's found the place, he's arranged a room for the night at a front counter. It's a nice building.

When Pete leads them back downstairs, he stops and asks the clerk. "Where can I buy jewelry, for a woman? …Not expensive."

At his odd request, the clerk looks Pete over. Jolan does the same. Both see Pete, all of sixteen, now in clean work clothes, but asking about jewelry. Neither laugh.

The clerk points outside, cool as anything. "One block south. Miller's Supply. Best place for that sort of thing." Looks at Pete's clothes again. "Just simple stuff. Probably what you're looking for."

"Thanks." This time it's Jolan, nodding with the invisible cap.

More marching around town. Finally, at least the inside of the supply store is interesting. Jolan runs his hand along the rakes, shovels, post-holers. And other tools, even swords. Candy too. But Pete leads them over to a counter with prettier things.

"I'm looking for something cheap." He tells the man behind the counter. "But nice, for a real lady."

First a quick smile. Then the man slowly loses that, as he gives Pete the hotel clerk's inspection all over again. "Yes, I think I have just the thing for you."

He reaches under the counter and brings out two earrings. Yellowy metal with little balls nestled like two black nest eggs.

"Here you are." Setting them on the counter, poking at the box they lay in with pride. "Gold plate, and local pearls. Irregular, but they look fine on your *lady's* neck."

Picking them up, Pete examines them, holding them up high. "And girls like these?"

The man nods. "Oh, yessir. Perfect for the price. The only other things I have are ten times as much."

And it dawns, though his weariness, Jolan's eyes snap from the baubles to Pete. "Eww, for Beneda?"

~~~

They've spent the day on small things, waiting. Trips to the stable, for Jolan to look at the mules and horses. Looking out their hotel window. Pete unwrapping and re-wrapping those earrings. *Like they migh a gone hidin' from him.* Jolan grins but won't tease…

And now, Pete, he say, "This should be good." Pete points at the empty table. They already ordered in this tavern.

"Gumbo!" Jolan licks his lips.

Pete smacks his lips. "Shrimp. Tomatoes. Rice. Okra."

"Don't like okra."

"But, you like gumbo."

Jolan thinks about it. "Yeah." There's celery, bell peppers, and onions. But the okra, that be slimy. "I
~~~

don’t like the okra on the plate. That stuff nasty. But, yeah, sure, if gumbo gots okra, I’ll eat it that way.”

Pete agrees, “That’s different.”

A woman hurries out of the kitchen, two bowls on her tray, and heading their way. Jolan sniffs like a dog as the steaming bowls come closer.

Grabbing up the spoon as soon as it sits before them, Jolan is stopped by Pete.

“What do you say?”

The younger boy bobs his head. “Thank you, ma’am.”

She swaps him with the edge of her cloth. “Enjoy!”

The hot stewy bowl keeps Jolan from finishing fast. He enjoys each bite. And wields the cornbread to soak up every last bit.

As he nears the bottom of the bowl, he notices Pete’s spoon’s stopped moving. Looking in the direction Pete stares, he sees a lady coming near their table. Jolan sees her mahogany face, her fancy dress. Shiny leather shoes peek out beneath a long swishy skirt. Old, maybe nineteen, maybe twenty years old.

Jolan's eyes follow her moving closer. Then, her eyes scan and stop at Pete. “Excuse me. Sir,” she says, lowered eyelashes against her cheeks. “May I sit here?”

“Y…Yes.” Pete stutters. “Of course.” It’s only Jolan who peeks around them at the other empty tables.

Sitting, the tips of her fingers on the table’s edge, shell-like nails, the thinnest of wrists, she asks, “I am looking for the farmers from Daufuskie Island,” she speaks breathlessly, offering a smile. Pete looks dumbstruck, *like he hit by lightnin’*. “We heard they are in town. My father sent me to find them. I'm Octavia." At that her eyes drop to those hands.

She reaches one out. Pete receives it more than stretches for it. Jolan thinks, *He droolin'!*

"I'm Pete," he answers low, his voice matching hers. His body leans across the table. Ignores the rest of his gumbo. And Jolan, beside him.

"Do you know the farmers?" She looks worried. "I need them." She tosses a glance, and then another, around the room, with a little worry in her frown.

Pete sputters out, "Ah—I am." Her face seems puzzled, at that until he adds, "I mean, I'm a farmer. *The farmers*."

Now, she smiles. Big. "Why, I'm so glad to find you." she whispers. Then hesitates.

"Good…" Pete seems at a loss. Even Jolan holds a mouthful of cornbread, no longer chewing.

"Do you have the papers?" Still speaking softly,

When she bats those lashes again, that's when Jolan goes back to his cornbread crusts.

"What?" Pete finally looks to Jolan. *He really confused,* Jolan figures.

"Do you have the papers? From the library?" Her voice more insistent now. Reminds Jolan of Old Lady Harris and his goose-bumps agree.

"Papers? No." Pete's answer comes abruptly.

At that, this Octavia, she leans back, graceful, reaching down, but holding a smile for Pete. Jolan, watches that hand. Those pearly nails. Like tracking a snake.

Her head tilts, those batty lashes working at gazing up straight into Pete's eyes. The older boy keeps staring, diving into those eyes.

Then, suddenly a small knife is in front of Pete's

nose. “I … need … those … papers.”

“Don’t have any…” Both Pete’s hands spread for her, wide empty.

Octavia’s face instantly becomes a smile again. As she rises, the knife vanished, she whispers again, “Goodbye.” Then smoothly she gone, up and out the door.

~~~

Walking over to a library bookcase under a window, Jolan steps over a sunlit square of floor. Books. In every direction. His eyes go to one with a red cover. It’s fat and tall in its stand. Glancing back into the room. he sighs, impatient at waiting again.

His gaze returns to that cover. Touching the red leather, he runs a finger down its edge. Follows ridges of letters. Pulling it from the others, he rubs it and opens it. The cover, hard. Like cardboard, mostly smooth, with small rough lines. A faint smell comes as the pages fall open.

“Be careful with that.” Pete calls over.

Almost dropping it, Jolan bristles. “I careful.” *You the one wif knifes in yo face.*

As the Librarian enters, robe swirling, Jolan sets the book down like it burns. He fumbles with placing it just like it was. Guiltily. Patting at it, back in its place.

With a smile at Jolan, then to Pete, she looks to the clock, gives him a moment to set it right. Then like all is tidy, she tells the boys, “We have the decision you wanted.”

Pete grins, Jolan figures, *he relieved. Don’t have to go back to Old Lady, empty handed*. “Thanks.”

“Librarian Oliver has recommended we hand
~~~

over the documents to you." Pete's happy nod is bright as the sun though the big window. "But, there is a condition."

Pete looks worried now. "Yas'um?"

"You must take them to the Bluffton Library. For safe keeping." She continues. "You understand? If there is a court case, it will happen there."

Bluffton? Pete gulps. First shaking his head, then nodding, shoulders down now. "Yas'um"

"Good. I will get them for you now." She waves for them to stay, as she turns. "And, there is someone I want you to meet." Her click-click of heels fades back down the hall.

Once she leaves, Jolan pipes up, "Bluffton? Ain't we goin' home?"

"Yeah. First to Bluffton, then home."

"Aw. Dats a long walk!"

Just that quick, the Librarian steps back in. No time to touch another book. Beside her, another well-dressed lady smiles at the boys.

"Pete, Jolan, this is Missus Chasseur." She points to the other, who nods to each boy. "Savannah is writing an article for the newspaper."

The other, this Missus Chasseur, she steps up to Pete and reaches her hand to shake. Jolan hears, "I have heard about the dispute around the land."

Pete looks at the librarian. Like he don't know if he should trust this new woman. Librarian Lincoln gives him a smile and a nod.

"Yas'um" Pete says, touching her hand in a quick shake. All Jolan knows is, *No knife so far.*

"I'd like to travel with you, to Bluffton."

Another nervous gulp from Pete. He cuts his eyes, quick, to Jolan. "Okay."

“I already have passage on the stage, tonight.” This Missus Chasseur, she brushes her hands down her spotless twill dress. “All ready for it. Join me, and I’ll pay your fare.”

A ride? Jolan bobs his head in time with Pete’s. “Thank you, Missus.”

Librarian Lincoln lifts a cloth bag, holding it up. *Mebbe they be food too*, Jolan hopes. Tight in her grip, she doesn’t hand it over yet. “Here are the papers.” Her eyes bore into Pete. “You know how important these are to your families?”

With a frown, Pete nods. Jolan thinks, *He gots to keep ‘em safe*. “Yas’um,” Pete vows, “*Ma’am*.”

“Well then,” she says, handing it over. Placing it solidly into Pete’s hands, she orders, “Put these into the hands of Librarian Oliver. No other.”

“Yas’um.” But Jolan notes, *Not a’nother somefin we be ‘ponsible fer!*

The librarian turns to the other woman. “Savannah. Have a pleasant journey. I look forward to reading all about it.”

“Goodbye, Gloria.” Hugging, this Missus Chasseur, she sighs. “Miss you. See you soon.” And it hits the boy, *‘theys friends!’*

Robe swirling, the librarian leaves, with a wave and one last word to the boys, “Don’t you let me down now.”

Examining Pete and Jolan, Missus Chasseur just has smiles to offer, no warnings, “Are you boys ready for the trip?”

Jolan nods as Pete packs the important bundle inside his travel-pack. It’s Pete who speaks up, “Yas’um. We ready.”

Gesturing for them to go on ahead, she strides to

the door behind them. Jolan thinks back on Beneda's mama goose and her goslings. In the lobby, this Missus Chasseur approaches the man at the desk.

"Preston." He's more than attentively watching her face. "Please send a message to Librarian Oliver. I would like some time with him for an interview. Tomorrow."

"Yes. Missus Chasseur." Again, Pete's eyes cut to Jolan. Though both boys stay mute.

Gripping her own handbag under her shoulder, she reaches for Pete and turns him to the door.

Jolan jumps at a slamming sound as the front door comes open before the trio has reached it. A man, carrying a muddy swamp smell to Jolan's nose, stops, just in the door. With eyes that stare directly at Pete, a goofy smile on his dark face. *Like they's friends too, but that can't be*, Jolan just hopes this one ain't got no new chore for them to do, too.

Jolan notices Pete shake a moment, before the other speaks, *nah, they ain't no friends. Nope.*

The goofy smile stops at this man's eyes as he calls, "Ah. You must be Pete Harris!"

Staring blankly, Pete steps back, more than a step, *Who be dis man? Why Pete so scairt?* But it's Missus Chasseur who's watching, between them, the woman reporter reaches toward Pete. Takes him right up under her wing, an arm on each shoulder. She asks low, "Pete, do you know this man?"

While his whole body shaking, he blurts, "No Ma'am!"

Inching closer, the man shows a still larger grin. "I am Cootuh." While he extends a hand, nobody puts theirs out. He focusing on Pete now. "I represent interests of those wanting to buy your farm."

Reaching in her bag, Missus Chasseur brings out a short pencil and a small pad of paper. She demands, "Who do you work for?"

"Eh… I work for *numerous interests, Ma'am*. Here son, is a letter." He hands it past Jolan. "Please deliver it to Beneda Washington," Directly on to Pete. As soon as Pete grabs it, with that blank look, the muddy swamp man turns and skips out the door.

15 Marsh Tacky - Warrior

The tables in front of the house are still up from the party. Missus Washington's table is mostly quiet. Just the sound of people slurping their morning's porridge. Beneda drinks milk, warm from the milking an bit ago. The smell helps wake her up. Caleb, her mama, Asante, Old Willy, and Turner set around the table. Lakisha, Nat, Angel, Tyrone, and Sarah at the next. All awaiting the papers to come from Beaufort.

"I miss Jolan." Caleb complains at the end of the table. "Wish I got t' go walkin'." His hand petting Aza.

Shining a stern expression on him, her mama scolds, "Hush Caleb. You brought it on yerself, eating like a pig."

Turning to Beneda, she confesses, "I miss them boys too. I worry."

"The library has pigeons at Bluffton." Asante speaks up. "Perhaps you can find what has happened with Pete and Jolan at Beaufort."

Beneda sees her mother is pleased at that information, though they'll need a runner to go there, and carry word back.

"Turner," Beneda asks. "Do you think you could ride to Bluffton? And inquire about the boys at that library?"

Nodding, he agrees, “Sure. My Marsh Tacky be fast and dependable.”

“Do you have another?” Asante inquires after this horse. “I think Lakisha should get back to her new job at the Bluffton Library, as well.”

When he nods, Asante calls out to the other table, “Lakisha— Turner here can carry you back to Bluffton. For work.”

Beneda wonders why he’d want that. “You sending her on to the Library?”

Asante shakes his head, no. “I mostly want to send the instructions with someone the Librarian’s already met.”

At that, Beneda’s mama rises and addresses Asante. “Scout. You’ll want to make a letter. For Turner and the girl to take.” This brooks no argument, Mama’s hand touches Turner’s wrist. “I fix some food up for your trip, Turner.”

Standing, Asante also brushes his hand over Beneda’s arm in passing. “Aza. Stay with Caleb.” Aza just twitches his ears as his head follows Asante moving to the house.

Smiling, Beneda’s next to rise. “You feeling right?” She asks Caleb. “Ready to go home?”

His head bobbing, his face lights up. “Yeah. Can Aza come too?”

“Maybe.” She warns, “I’ll have to check with the scout.”

“Beneda, you g’on.” Old Willy says. “The crop almost all in. We finish today or tomorra.” Waving over to the other table, “Wif alla de hands a body could want. We’all gots dis. You can take de time off.”

Nodding, her smile beams on him, her eyes

follow the scout who's moving into the house.
"Thanks Willy. I will travel to Old Lady Harris' place, with Caleb. See how she doing."

~~~

It was a walk. Just lucky for the cloud cover, such as it is. Now, Beneda's sweating, as she and the others help get in the last of the corn in for Old Lady Harris. Caleb helps by carrying empty sacks. Aza stays at the boy's side, watching the little one. Glancing over, Beneda studies Asante, picking. His thumb near the top of the head, his fingers near the bottom, then a sharp downward pull. She thinks, *he doing good for just starting*.

"Pick de ones with dark silks." Old Lady reminds him, she could boss a hog into a barbecue pit.

Nodding at her instructing, the scout keeps working, he sweats too.

Beneda calls out to Old Lady, "Lakisha and Turner be riding to Bluffton. Gon' ask about your grandboy, and Jolan."

"Good." The old woman nods, hands on hips. "He a good boy. Pete do what right."

At the end of the day, they all rest and Old Lady Harris becomes the hostess with drinks of lemonade for all, and shortbread slathered with butter, too. Gathered at the front porch Caleb sits with Aza in the shade, the pup gets his share of the bread, as the scents of supper come wafting from the cookhouse. Old Lady sits on the stoop, wooden needles flashing in her hands as she knits. Beneda examines her bow and fletching on her arrows. M'Deah had said, *keep*
~~~

the shafts and bow ready.

On a grassy area nearby, Asante stretches and from a standing start, he shifts down and back upright, moving in awkward looking poses that make Beneda blush to watch.

"Yoga?" she calls over to him.

He doesn't break the pose, holds it a bit before calling, "Egyptian yoga." With a smile, "From ancient hieroglyphics."

Caleb calls out. "I want to do that." Then he tumbles, head over heels, as Aza watches.

Asante laughs, turning back to Beneda. "Just as you prepare your bow, I must prepare *my* weapon."

Smiling she notices his glance strays to the road. Eyes shaded, she spies horses turning up the path and steps away from Old Lady Harris' side on the porch. As the newcomers move closer, she recognizes Turner on his Marsh Tacky, leading a second one.

Old Lady squints. "Turner must be back from the Library."

Beneda sets her arrows away and steps over as the horses trot up. Waving to Caleb, she grasps the reins of one. As Caleb hops over, Turner dismounts and staggers for a moment, from the all-day ride.

Bowing to Old Lady, "Miss Harris, yo' grandson be in Bluffton." To Beneda. "And Jolan."

"Thanks." Beneda smiles and pats at the thin Marsh Tacky, she calls out to Caleb pulling the other, "Bring em on." After leading the sweaty horses to the water trough, Caleb starts in with a curry comb.

The man, Turner, is puffing from his ride. Asante's stopped the yoga to come join them, but Turner, he moves on to Beneda.

"Beneda. This here a letter. Pete, said it be

important." Pausing for a breath, hands on the small of his back. "From Cootuh."

A growl rumbles in her throat, as she leaves the horses with Caleb and walks back to the shade of the porch.

Not meaning to, she finds she's snatched the envelope from Turner, and wipes her hands before ripping it open. After a moment's read she hands it to Asante.

In an instant, his eyes rise to hers in surprise. "What will you do?"

"I have to go."

Old Lady taps her needles together. "What it be, girl?"

Waving at the letter, Beneda calls up to her. "Cootuh writes he will show me the papers that claim our land."

"Cain't trust 'em," the old lady insists.

"I know, but…" Beneda pauses, choosing her words carefully, she explains to Old Lady, "Cootuh held me once. But didn't hurt me. Seems to me this is important enough that I'll have to go. It's me he's asking for."

"We have to keep you safe." Asante nods to Old Lady, then to Turner, deciding just that quick. "I'll go with her." He waves the page she's handed over. "We don't have much time."

Nodding, Beneda heads up the porch steps to Old Lady. "It's today. Can we borrow horses?"

"Sound dangerous?" Lady Harris gives Beneda a hard look, but asks only that.

Beneda thinks she's right, but. "We have no choice…"

Still, with worry on her face, Old Lady's stopped

the knitting, placing it in her lap. "What I tell your mama? If'n you come t' harm?"

Beneda tries to come up with the right answer. "When you and M'Deah defended the farms…" holding the older one's eyes. "You had to make hard decisions."

"Of course, Beneda." Old Lady finally nods. "You watch yourself."

"Should we take Aza?" Beneda wonders.

"No. I suspect, that Cootuh might think I'd use him to track him. Like we tracked you the first time. Besides, with Caleb on the mend, Aza can do best keeping him company." Asante comments, then waves to Turner.

Turner wipes sweat off his brow. "I'd come. But my Marsh Tackys done for the day, but you gots a horse what we can use? Mines ain't got no distance left."

~~~

The trio crouch in bushes looking into a clearing. Spanish Moss hangs down from the trees over their heads. Asante's arm rests on Beneda's shoulder, keeping her down. On her left Turner studies the clearing, ignoring how the scout's arm sets. She thinks Asante's hand feels warm and comfortable there next to her quiver of arrows.

"What do you think?" Beneda wonders.

"I only see three of them." To Turner, the scout whispers, "If we had more people, I'd want to do a proper scout of the area."

Beneda wishes she'd changed to something right for stalking this way. But only asks, "Can we do that?" She worries, there's Cootuh out there, and two
~~~

other folks she's never laid eyes on. *An even match if it came to that*, but what if more are lurking in the trees beyond?

Shaking his head, the scout thinks on that for second. The other two wait. "No time."

"I miss your dog."

"Yes. Aza's my shadow." Shaking his head, Asante continues, still in a low profile. "Might as well go meet them now."

"Can we trust them?" Beneda feels worried now, she doesn't think to rise yet. But does question whether to leave her bow with Turner or not.

"No." Asante shakes his head. "But we shall hope they have an interest in us walking away from this." Thinking a moment, then tilting his head to Turner, a final decision comes, "You stay back from us. Near the trees. If we're taken, go get help."

With a gulp, Turner nods.

Beneda looks into Asante's eyes. He touches her hand. She stands, tells him, "Now. For my farm."

"*Cootuh*." Her voice rings with accusation.

"Miss Washington." Bowing his head, like she's royalty. "This is Octavia. And, Jeremiah."

Beneda thinks the woman would stand out in any crowd. *Has means, knows how to wear what it's bought her*. Spotless slacks, trim denim blouse and a fringed vest. Browns and tans highlight her face and hair. Now Beneda's glad she didn't change after all.

She tries imprinting their faces. "You invited us to meet here. The middle of nowhere. Why?"

After Cootuh waves to his partner, the spotless woman pulls papers from her vest.

"I wanted to share this with you." There's something in that voice. Holding it out, she doesn't deign to move closer to Beneda. Just waits for the papers to leave her outstretched hand. "This proves we own your farms."

Mentally wrestling, *Why you—* Beneda hesitates. But taking the chance, she decides and is moving forward. With a glance over to Asante, she takes the paper. Noticing Asante hasn't moved, Beneda scans what's now in her hand. Three pages. One old page. Another, some affidavit. The last, a judge's ruling. It doesn't mean much to her. She half turns, eyes still on this woman, holding the pages back toward the scout.

She stares into her face, this *Octavia*. Seeing a faint smile there, it worries Beneda. Asante's taken the papers. Beneda ignores his shuffling through them, instead watching these three before her.

With a slap of the pages, Asante speaks to the trio now. "These mean nothing." He's come forward, standing shoulder to shoulder with Beneda. "This judge's ruling will have no power over the farmers. The case will have to be retried in a local court."

Beneda watches Octavia's face, as that smile grows wide. Her right hand rises up over her head. With a snap of her pale fingers, movement from the woods behind the three draws Beneda's eyes. *More men!* Asante grabs her arm, too late, she notices Cootuh looks shocked, turning toward Octavia.

"Let's go." Asante urgently tugs her away from the center of the field. Turning her brain off, Beneda moves to follow.

The ground is rough. On their sprint back to Turner she focuses to avoid tripping. He's faded into the woods ahead of them.

Stopping behind the trees, they reach Turner, who asks, “The horses?”

Looking out at those approaching. Asante’s head shakes, hard. “No. They’ll cut us off.” Pointing north, away from where they’re tethered, he asks, “What’s that way?”

“Small abandoned town.” Turner waves up the barely visible path, they’re aware of the noise behind. “’bout a kilometer.”

“Let’s go.” Asante moves.

Beneda has a hard time keeping up. Asante seems more sure footed. She knows Turner’s hasn’t done this in years. Hearing shouts behind her speeds her, a little.

Turner gasps out, “How many?”

“I counted ten. And the woman.” He slows a fraction. “I saw one bow.”

Continuing, a little slower now, Beneda knows Turner struggles like her.

Pacing her run next to him, she sputters, “How far?”

“’nother minute…mebbe…”

Pitching her voice forward to Asante, “Then what?”

“We hide,” comes from the scout. Sure and decisive. More steps. “Where they can only come at us one at a time.”

He could keep this up for hours, Beneda thinks, *he doesn’t sound winded at all.* Glancing to Turner, she doubts the two of them could.

Ahead she sees a crumbling shack. Then more, all broken down. Asante points, while still moving fast. A taller one, *maybe a church?* They follow as he speeds up for that goal. Turner and Beneda fall behind. Seconds later, they arrive at a half-collapsed stone and wood church, where Asante waits.

Pointing, to Beneda he orders, "Inside. We'll stand here."

Beneda scurries over dusty stone steps. Doves fly out from the roof opened to the sky. Asante heads directly to a staircase to the side. *Belltower?*

Beneda follows the scout up the steps. But stops as she notices Turner isn't behind.

"Turner?"

Shaking his head. "I leads dem off."

"But—"

He pulls his big knife out. "I won't be good in a fight." Waving it at Asante. "If'n they follow, chasing me can tire em out."

Beneda's eyes move to Asante. Pleading. He's moved back down several of the rickety steps. His face not moving as his hands grip her shoulders.

Beneda's lip quivers, "But—"

"Miss Beneda, tell Miss Bessie, I sorry." Turner steps to the door. "If'n they leave me alone, I'll double back an' take the horses to the next town. Wait fer y'all der."

He steps out, as Beneda shakes in the scout's hands.

"Honor him." He whispers in her ear, "His sacrifice means time."

In anger and frustration, shaking her head, Beneda turns, facing the scout. "Yes. Of course. What do we do?"

"We hide."

They climb higher. Amid the dust and crumbled bricks. At a window, Beneda spies figures moving. Browns and darker homespun blending into the trees.

Turner's outside the wrecked town now, his gait hard to miss, moving fast. But those figures seem to be gaining.

No! Turner's down. Picking their way through a formerly tilled field, Beneda can't see it all now, but it must be an arrow. She turns away as more attackers reach the ground Turner's stopped at.

Must not cry. Asante leads her further up. Stopping at a side room, he examines it. *Won't be able to use my bow well.*

Waving her in, he points to a small bookcase across the room. "There. You have two meters to shoot. Hide. If anyone comes in stop them."

He squeezes her arm then steps out, turning right to go up even higher. Beneda sets her quiver against the case. Counting, twelve arrows. She sits, hugging her bow to her and waits.

In minutes, shouting comes from below on the stairs. Sounds move closer. *Climbing.* She gets up in a crouch, ready.

"You see anything?" *She knows that voice. The redhead, Brutha.*

"No. Maybe they ain't here."

"Keep lo—"

A sudden crash.

A shout and next Beneda fears someone's made it up to this room. Rising as Brutha takes another step in, searching, turning, and breathing hard from the climb as she had. Without thinking, she releases. Her arrow strikes. High, just behind his shoulder. He bats at it like swatting at flies out of reach. It stays embedded. He doesn't slow, though hurt. His howls tell her that.

Another shout, and Asante is back in the narrow hallway outside her room. Two swordsmen rush him. One, no shirt and a leather vest. The other in a dirty white shirt. In a flurry of swings, Asante moves through the door, and they pursue; around the room. Cutting his enemies, he bests one. In seconds his back is toward Brutha, who's stopped trying for the arrow. Still. He raises his club, stepping forward on wobbly legs.

Cursing, Beneda quickly looses two more arrows, Brutha's thigh and kidney. Then, he turns. Another strikes his gut. He keeps coming at her. Another arrow, then a step back. As she reaches for another, he staggers to his knees. Thinking, *seven more*, she nocks it.

Brutha's look stuns her. It seems one of betrayal. Finally, dropping his club, he crumbles. Looking up she sees Asante. No one else remains standing.

Movement at the door. With a cry, Hector, the slow one from the cabin, jumps into the room. His eyes go to Brutha face-down, fletchings rising from his body. Then to the others sprawled, still. Then, his eyes, darting like fish, move to first Asante then Beneda. She reads hurt and pain. Slowly he raises his club.

"Stop!" Asante shouts.

Hector does just that for a second, then takes another step. With a loud whack, the scout knocks him in the head. No blood, it was no hacking move. Hector staggers, turning back to Asante. Again, the sword flat is laid against this one's head, with a crack filling the room this time. As Hector falls to his knees, Beneda notices Asante's expression.

She sees him, maybe for the first time. And reading those eyes, understands the generosity of the scout's soul. There's a depth of compassion, there in those eyes. A wave of emotion washes over her and she tries recognizing what she feels.

In a small voice she offers, "Thank you, his name's Hector. *Forgive him,*" she whispers, hoping she's used the right words to express the respect she feels for this man from Africa.

Around the disarrayed room, Beneda finds herself wishing more men were like Asante. She's beginning to measure other's behavior against him. She hadn't been sure how she felt about him. Glancing at Hector, she sees the recipient of Asante's mercy this day.

It isn't difficult finding herself wanting to gaze longer into Asante's eyes, to search in those depths for shared feeling. The thought that those eyes might be closed forever sends a chill through her.

Staggering for an instant, she reaches out to steady herself against the bookcase. Takes a deep breath, reaching inside herself for the resolve to make sure they don't die today.

Soon her face is locked in determination and her hands steady. She regards Hector once more. Beneda's mind works fast and sure, makes a list; *enlist allies, get horses, find Turner, return to Mama!*

Stepping to stand over the kneeling figure, she puts her hand on his shoulder. The scout moves to the door.

"Hector!" Before her, his eye swim trying to focus. "We need your help. Will you please help me, Hector?"

Nodding a slow yes causes Hector's hand to rise, fingertip to a growing blueish bruise. Then he seems to see her.

"What?"

"Please, Hector. I need you to help me." Staring in his eyes, she grabs his hands and demands, "Will you help?"

He glances around the room once, then back into Beneda's eyes. "Yes."

16 Comfort - Warrior

On the hilltop above the family farm, Beneda feels glad for the near silence. Only the faint croaking of the leopard frogs, by the stream, comes to her ears. Though the grunts and slashing of the fight visit her in a waking dream.

"Beautiful basket." Asante's words come softly, as she looks down on her house below.

"It's coiled grass." Beneda's voice is hoarse and husky. "I sat at M'Deah's feet, as she guided my hands in making these sweetgrass baskets." She feels the grass of the basket with her hand, but stares below at Bessie, Marquetta and the others moving below, around the rough wooden coffin.

Following her eyes, he asks, "She cared for Turner? Miss Bessie?"

Her body swaying from emotion, guilt wracks her mind. It's all Beneda can do when she admits, "Yes." Beneda remembers the response as she offered her arms and comfort. Bessie's words, *'When you face them again, I will help you. Anything you need of me!'*

Using a small knife, she cuts some Yellow Jessamine. Placing them into the basket in bunches, she tries not to think about Turner's coffin down there.

"Your friends love you."

She glances up to this scout's face. Notices a small scar on his cheek, but only thinks to herself, *I can't fix it. I can't change it*. For a fleeting moment she wonders how he got such a memento. She wants to know more about the man beside her.

"Yes. Friends." Stroking the Jessamine in her hand. "They keep me from despair."

"You made the right choices." The scout reaches over to touch her arm.

"I think so," softly. "But, I have to live with them." A tear drops down her cheek.

"You are their leader." Asante moves even closer now, he loses his words for a moment.

"Does it ever get easier?"

Grasping her arms, his voice rasps out, "You don't want it to." His hand tightens. "Don't ever forget why you do it." Squeezes. "Why you act."

So near now, she notices his eyes, not as completely brown as from a distance. There are specks of green in there. Raising the flowers to cover her face, *should I even do this?*

"The farm, family, and friends." Smiling through her tears. But her heart's still heavy.

His finger brushes her cheek, moving the flowers from her face. Tracing the library symbol on his vest she wonders, *how far has he traveled to be here today?* With his hands tracing the skin on her arms, she feels his hesitation.

As he pulls her closer, she feels his beating heart. Her eyes narrowing to slits, she leans into those arms.

She stops holding back, and impulsively kisses this scout.

~~~
~~~

This impromptu memorial bakes under an intense morning sun. Beside Beneda, Marquetta waits near the long plank benches, lined up for mourners. Beneda's overwhelmed, by smells from flowers everywhere in front of the house.

"Your scout performing dis service?"

"Turner's son asked Asante."

"How you two doin'?" *Even today she can't help teasing me.* Beneda turns her burning face away. But it doesn't help. Marquetta murmurs, "Something happened!"

Beneda softly confesses, "Yes." Marquetta bounces, like a spring tied down and straining.

"What happen? D'you kiss?" At Beneda's tiny nod, Marquetta grabs at her arm. "*Girl!*"

"Marquetta."

"Beneda."

Shrugging her arm away, Beneda hisses low, "Sss—speak later." Brushing her friend's arm, she points at Turner's son approaching. Marquetta takes on a more serious face, calms down.

Young Turner leans on his crutch, saying, "Thank you Beneda, for holding my father's memorial at your place."

Beneda's shiny, red-rimmed eyes meet his. "Mama and I wanted to honor him." Blinking, she struggles. "He gave his life. For mine."

She watches how his jaw clenches, the tightened grip on his crutch. "I know. Proud'a him." She sees he doesn't want her apology. Still, Young Turner is his father's son, he adds, "I and everyone on the Brown farm appreciates—your work for us."

Remembering what Asante told her, *accept it, lead.* She dips her chin, saying, "Thank you, and them."

Before he steps away, the boy says, "You're doing a good job with the library scout."

"Yes?" Her ears get hot, from his words, and more. She ignores Marquetta rubbing softly at her arm.

Turner waves to the fields of trampled corn stocks. "To save this we need the libraries' help"

Beneda's face relaxes into a weak grin. "Yes. But, we need to help ourselves, too."

Bessie besides the coffin, and Asante, wave Young Turner over. With a nod to Beneda he moves away on his crutch. She thinks, *I should be making plans*. Thinks, *what's at stake*. But her mind can't focus on any one thing.

Marquetta holds onto her arm again. "You don't have to be embarrassed." Softly in her ear.

Need to switch topics. Her friend knows her too well. To drag her mind from the kiss, Beneda straightens her spine and shakes the big girl's hand off. "We have to get ready. Work to protect the farms. Make plans, now."

Marquetta ignores her words, patting her hand, whispers, "He'll join us after the ceremony."

As Asante raises his arms, Beneda's mind returns to the present. As the talking quiets, people settle down. They turn toward him beside the fresh wooden box.

"Welcome family and friends to this celebration of a good life."

A few shift, and settle in, many, so many, wipe at their eyes. And the scout goes on, "Turner did not live his life alone. He has been loved and cared for by you, his family, and friends. He depended on you for sustenance, knowledge, guidance, and love. Without you, he wouldn't have been the man we've known him to be…"

Beneda's mind splinters between the present, the battle at the church, and her time on the hill with the scout. *Why can't I settle on one thought?*

"Friends, family. Today we say goodbye to Turner. You were fortunate to have him in your lives. He was truly blessed to have your love and affection…"

Does our life save those around us, or endanger them? she worries. "… here, and thank each of you for coming to share this very special ti…." Beneda's eyes track to Bessie, silently crying up front, Old Lady Harris holding her tight.

"…must leave the people you love; lives you share…" She tries to smile. "…beyond our power. Honor that love…"

At this, Beneda lets a sigh escape. "Let's have a few moments in silence. But as we begin, I ask each of you to recall a time that you shared with Turner that you'd like to keep in your minds and hearts. It can be something insignificant, maybe a smile, or a moment shared you like remembering. Now we'll have that moment of silence…"

Those words, Beneda can't stop thinking about who says them. This library scout, Asante, here, laying a friend to rest, gathering up her heart. But, where will he be tomorrow?

"Today, you take a separate path. No longer with him. You have known him for years, through first acquaintance to this moment…"

He's done this before.

Marquetta whispers into Beneda's ear, "Asante

write dis ceremony?"

"With Bessie, and Turner's son," she whispers back. Beneda thinks about the future. *What needs to be done?* Check on papers in Bluffton, get Jolan back, and Pete, and figure out *her* with *Asante*. Beneda's list.

"Go in peace, and honor his memory."

At these words, Beneda stands a bit taller. She feels wetness on the back of her hand. She glances to find Marquetta's red eyes.

17 Consequences- Trickster

Cootuh shakes in anger, biting his tongue at Octavia tending her plants. *Cares more for them flowers than those we still need to bury.* The greenhouse seems bright with light. Trying to calm his thoughts he counts the window panes, and contemplates the vast cost displayed by this small building.

"Those were our men," comes forced out between gritted teeth.

"It is important to move fast." Her lips quirk up, ignoring his words. "In a month, we will miss the growing season."

Cootuh tries and fails to control his trembling. *She don't think about the people.* They can't win by making more enemies, but he can't say that.

"You don't know fighting." Trying to stay respectful, Cootuh tries his best. His hat in his hand gets the squeeze he'd like to give her neck. "You know that, right?"

Octavia's smile disappears. "Yes, I understand."

Breathing deeply, he turns aside for a moment. Purple flowers to his left grab his attention. He reaches over…

"Don't touch that!" Her shout freezes him. "Wolfsbane…" *Guess she cares, sometimes*. "Don't touch that with bare hands."

"Hobby?"

Returning to trimming, she's turned her back now, throws over her shoulder, "I like the orderliness of my garden." With a wave around the room. "Everything in place, a job for everything. I love them."

Cootuh looks around. *This place* is *special, ordered rows, like to like.* There is Oleander, Foxglove, Nightshade, Lilly of the Valley… *Maybe not just a hobby.*

Pointing to a little pot holding a stunted tree, Octavia boasts, "My prized one." With a beaming face, she points to its gnarled little branches. "A bonzai Hemlock. Isn't it beautiful?"

Cootuh waggles his head, not agreeing or disagreeing. He'd like to know about her feeling toward people. He waves at the door. "Why do you hate them?"

"I don't hate anyone." Dimples show on her cheeks with her faint smile. "I want to help them."

His lips become taut. "Your approach is dangerous."

"Because I care, I want what's best for them." Reminds Cootuh of her father. Octavia's like her plants, no awareness or concern of the world outside.

"I guess." Cootuh hopes she won't surprise him again. Like she done before. "We'll have to convince them. Of what's best."

Waving at the neat rows of deadly plants. Octavia proclaims, "People need to be organized. Or useful."

~~~

Sitting with Octavia at a large table, Cootuh
~~~

examines a map she's spread across it, plans for all the property they expect to have. As Malcolm enters, Cootuh loses his train of thought; his hand comes up from the map.

"Got a letter from you father, Miss Octavia." Only a small scowl crosses his lips when he glances at Cootuh. "He's delayed. You're to take charge until he returns."

Her eyes opening wide, she smiles. "Of course! I want to deal with those Gullah farms." The news spreads that smile, falling on both these men. At least for a moment.

Malcolm tosses a smile back at her, ready to prove himself. "Be great if we can solve that before Mister Buckra returns."

Cootuh informs them, "The official legal documents are all moved to Bluffton."

Moving a manicured hand toward Cootuh, she asks, "Can your contact get them for us?"

Shaking his head, he loses the smile he has for her, forced to say, "No. Oa—m-my contact is getting harder to work with."

Malcolm jumps on that; he suggests, with eyes on Miss Octavia, "Well, we will just have to go in ourselves."

Cautious, she studies her map, then Cootuh. Finally, with brow low, Octavia asks, "Is the library well defended?"

Cootuh strokes his chin, he hesitates, but has to admit. "No. Only one guard at night, same during day. Sure, it's a big building, lots of wings. And grounds. But no, not well defended."

Octavia leans back in her chair, satisfied at that, a finger lingers on the map's edge. Maybe even glad her papa's out and away. "That scout seemed very dangerous."

Cootuh sighs, "We don't have to worry. Someone's going to rid us of that problem." When Octavia's eyes dart to him. He simply adds, "It won't be traced back to you."

Turning her attention to Malcolm, it's with a relieved look that she demands, "Organize a group to go to Bluffton and take the papers from the library." She waits. Thinking, then that smile once again. "How much time do we have before planting must begin?"

Cootuh looks across the table at Malcolm for his opinion.

"A little over a month before we can get the crop planted."

She wonders, "Do we *have* to start planting in June?"

"No. But we need three to six months of steady sun for rice." Malcolm cautions, then he continues, "If we start later we may need to start seeding here in seeding beds, transporting to the fields later."

"When will we want to start the Indigo planting?"

"About three months before winter for it to reach harvest time."

Cootuh cuts in, "I'm continuing recruiting." She like it when he speaks his best, "We will have almost a full crew for the ten farms in a month."

"So—you got some fellows now?" Malcolm stares intently at Cootuh. "You can take a group. You must get those papers."

Octavia looks down at their plans, laid out so perfectly on the wide table, she next reminds Cootuh, "Don't fail us again."

18 Farewell - Warrior

In her home, Asante reaches out and touches Beneda's arm. "Speaking of, I probably should return to the Bluffton Library…"

Beneda's mind races, until she remembers, "I wanted to introduce you to more farmers."

She looks to her other guest. After Turner's funeral, Old Lady remained with Beneda. Happy to sit a while in the comfortable chair, in the Washington home, embroidering a patch she's mended on a pair of Caleb's denim pants. Her needle adds a few more useless stitches, as she cuts her eyes at the scout, here beside Beneda. Who wonders how she sees the pair off by the big window, chatting. Running into the room, Caleb shouts, breaking that train of thought.

"What'ya put'n on dem." he demands.

Old Lady grins, snapping off a thread with her teeth. "I'ma put'n on a goat."

"I wants a dog. Like Aza."

Sighing, Old Lady agrees. "Okay, lil'n."

Running out the room, Caleb shouts, "Yay!" with as much commotion as possible, Aza follows, hot on the boy's heels.

Beneda grins at Old Lady, "I'm glad you and Caleb decided to stay."

Old Lady's face wrinkles up more with humor. "I

want t' visit more with y' mama." Shaking ruefully. "Well, I bide, till she back from tak'n Bessie home."

The scout now studies Beneda's eyes. Gently, he says, "I have delivered the papers. I should report back to the Librarian."

Old Lady speaks up, "Beneda, maybe you could go to Bluffton. Check up on my Pete."

Beneda beams for a moment, thanking Old Lady with her eyes. "Yas'um." In a lower tone, she adds, "I'll travel with you."

Asante squeezes her hand. "Good." Those eyes kindly study Beneda. Then they shift to Old Lady at her needle.

Old Lady softly coos, "You be needing to write up pages for de Librarian?" At his smile and nod she sets Caleb's pants aside and waves a gnarled hand toward mama's writing desk. "Have at it. Beneda, help me in the kitchen. Gots to get you some'm for the road."

First, watching Old Lady make her way to the door, Beneda then gives a quick peck to Asante's cheek, softly. "See you."

Following Old Lady out the room and to the kitchen, Beneda wonders *What will mama think?*

Grabbing a stalk of celery and a knife, Old Lady spares a glance at Beneda. "What y' want me to tell y' mama, girl?"

It's just business. Tell her that. A few chops, the only noise in the kitchen, then, "I'll be back in a few days."

"Fetch me a bag, fer the food." As Beneda pulls an old worn travel pack from a cupboard, Old Lady aims a second glance, sharp as her needle. "What y' want me to tell her about the *Scout*?"

Catching that meaning, and the gleaming in her eyes, Beneda tries thinking of what Old Lady has seen of her and Asante. *Maybe a little handholding?*

"I will accompany him to Bluffton." Beneda offers, as innocently as she can. Smoothing out the sack in her hands.

"Don't play dumb wit me, child." The old one scowls. "M'Deah had me watch y' mama like a hawk when she was seeing y' papa."

Shocked at the story she hadn't heard, Beneda chokes. "Uh. I'ma ask Marquetta to come to Bluffton wit us."

"That girl be silly. You need t' watch that one."

"She my friend." *Wooly headed, but still…*

"You take'n horses?"

Beneda thinks on it. After a moment, thinks *yes*. "I don't like the expense, and worry. But, we might need to move in a hurry. We'll take three."

Old Lady examines the light left in the day, looking out the kitchen window. "Y'all best get a move on. Make Bluffton by nightfall. Tell Pete to send Jolan home. I know y' mama miss dat child."

~~~

By nightfall, they've finally reached Bluffton. "*Just*," Marquetta complains to Beneda. Sitting there with Jolan, and Pete in the tavern, she and Beneda sip lemonade.

Pete speaks up even with a mouthful of cornbread. "I think somebody need t' stay near de library."

Biting her lips, Beneda knows that may be true. And that she should have thought it herself. She asks him, "What can you do, if there's trouble?"
~~~

Pete frowns, down at his lemonade. “Don’t know”

Marquetta offers. “I’ll take Jolan home. Tomorra. One less thing to *worry on,* Beneda.”

Jolan misses what she means, he only pipes up. “I wants t’ stay. And fight.”

Marquetta swats him on the head and Jolan leans over to Pete, for protection. Beneda’s thinking, *it’s cute how the boys have become close on this trip*.

Seeing Marquetta’s staring toward the door, Beneda glances over. Her heart races to see Asante striding in, heading for their table. Then it thuds to a stop at the expression on his face.

Walking up and greeting folks, his eyes settle on Beneda. *Serious.*

“Beneda.” As their eyes meet he requests, “Let’s go outside.”

Her heart thumps a few bumpy beats but she gets up. Avoids looking at the others. She wants to avoid knowing whatever look be on Marquetta’s face.

Outside, the last bit of sunset doesn’t mean the heat’s gone. Light may be near faded, but the hot remains. Asante grasps her hand. He looks about to speak. Beneda has never seen him hesitate. Well, except for one time.

“Beneda.” A pause. “I’m being sent back to Africa.”

Beneda feels rocked back on her heels. “But.” *Why now?* “Can you refuse?”

His eyes stare deeply into hers. Then dart away. Then back. “I can quit.”

Swallowing with a gulp, she tries to think. He

loves the libraries. “When do you leave?” Not wanting to hear the answer. “And Aza?”

“Aza’s with Lakisha. They’ll travel with me. Right away. Librarian Oliver—he’s already purchased the ticket. I know Jolan and Caleb will miss Aza.” Shaking his head, a look on his face she can’t decipher. “The clipper to Africa. Leaves tomorrow from Port Wentworth.”

Her hand going to her mouth. “No…”

His eyes bright, “I know,” looking down into hers. “I don’t want to go.” That makes her feel better, but, not much, *Why? Why couldn’t they be somewhere private?*

So hard to get out words, Beneda struggles to control her emotions. “Why.” No one should see her like this, especially him. “Why the rush to leave?”

Asante ventures, “I wonder that also.” His eyes straying back up the street, *Casting back to the meeting he’s come from?* “You might tell your friends to keep a watch on the library. Where the papers are.”

That distracts her. Thinking an instant she makes a list, *say goodbye, plan, save the farms, cry later.* Reaching, she grabs his vest with both hands. Pulling herself to his chest, she cleaves her lips to his.

The couple clasp together, ignoring people walking past. Opening her mouth, she thinks, *give him something to remember on the long journey.*

Finally, she loosens his vest and pulls back. Shaking her head, slowly aware of those others on the street, some gawking, Beneda thinks about her list. “Come.” Waving him back into the tavern. “Tell the others. About defending the papers.”

Nodding, Asante follows. Their hands grip tightly together until they cross the threshold. Then, they let them fall, walking to the table, all eyes on them. Beneda notices Jolan's stare, eyes as wide as saucers.

Stopping together in front of them, Beneda makes the scout's announcement, "Asante is leaving. Today."

Marquetta's mouth drops. "No." She looks about to blurt something more, but Beneda gives her friend a stare.

"He has an important warning about the library." That works to get Pete and Marquetta focused.

Briefly Asante meets each of their eyes, serious as a heart attack. "I am suspicious of my orders to leave. So suddenly." Thinking a moment, lips pursed for a moment before speaking, "I can only advise that —perhaps, you keep a watch on the library tonight."

Marquetta nods, then to Beneda she frowns. Saying, "But. Asante. Don't go." Trust her to speak Beneda's mind, she struggles to keep her eyes from going misty.

"Miss Marquetta, Pete, Jolan, I regret leaving you all." He touches Beneda's hand. "I will miss you more than you can know. May your lives be full. May you find happiness and success."

Pete looks between Beneda and the scout. Squaring his shoulders, he offers a simple, "Pleasant journey, Mister Asante."

Beneda turns to Asante. His eyes and hands find hers. She memorizes the look of his lips. Thinks, *he's struggling, to stay or go.*

Yet, he slowly releases her hands, turns and walks away.

~~~

In the moonlight, Beneda and Marquetta now sit
~~~

on a park bench. Beneda's eyes on the entrance across the lawn, to the library; she uses her fingers examining her arrows. Eleven. After losing one, the day Turner died.

Marquetta points to her bow. "You killed people with that?"

"Only one." Beneda thinks of Brutha. How she knew him. Didn't like him, but knew him.

"That must been such a fight." There's an excited sound in Marquetta words. Beneda doesn't remember it that way.

"It was scary and tiring."

"Tiring?" The big girl leans back at this, the bench groans.

"We began by running." She meets Marquetta's surprise with a rueful half-smile. In the dimness, that smile becomes wider as Beneda remembers the scouts words, 'many battles are won by fast running!'

"We ran so hard. Like when we were young and chased after imaginary fairies in the woods."

Marquetta's laugh falls into a new silence, then she whispers, "Do you think anyone will come tonight?"

Beneda glances up at the moon. "If it's Cootuh… it'll be around midnight."

Nodding, with a frown Marquetta thinks out-loud, "It be scary how you can think like that fool."

"I remember M'Deah saying, 'keep all y' enemies close.'"

"Forget y' enemies. Why you send Asante away?" After a glare, Marquetta tries again, that stubborn girl. "I know. You grab de scrawny librarian by he neck. Demand he call the scout back."

"Marquetta…"

"It what I do!"

"I know." Beneda gives a knowing nod. She's seen Marquetta's courting style.

"If'n it were y' mama." Marquetta gives a smirk, like she an expert on this here topic. "She'd serve the librarian tea an' say, 'Please, sir, Mister Librarian, would you be so good as to inquire into the manner of recalling the good scout Asante, from the distant continent of Africa?'"

Casting an angry frown her way, Beneda points at the fullness of the moon. "Remember. Midnight."

Looking around the shadowy area before the building, Marquetta decides and stands. "I'll check on Pete. In back."

Her friend disappears around the side of the building, Beneda, mind elsewhere, checks her bow again. Till the sound of snapping twigs moves her to nock her arrow, stand, and turn in one fluid motion. She thinks, *ten in the quiver*.

There, before her stands Cootuh, his empty hands raised.

Behind him, two men, one with a sword, the other carrying a club. They wait a meter back.

"Cootuh." Her voice comes dripping with accusation.

"Ah, Miss Beneda. So good to see you again."

Keeping the arrow pointed at his neck, she thinks, *I can nock and release twice more*. Probably not quick enough.

"We won't let you get our papers." It's really all she has against these three.

"Surely, they are the libraries' papers."

"Don't be clever."

"I was sorry to hear your scout friend has left."

Beneda detects no sorrow in that voice, but a slice of guile in those words does reach her.

"Bless your heart, you have something to do with that?" Accusation in her voice.

His men can't see it, but Cootuh's face takes on an exaggerated look of shock. "Why I neve…"

She dismissed that, when the sound of a voice—*Pete?* Comes from behind her. A shout. With a last glance at Cootuh and his two thugs, Beneda grabs her quiver and takes off running.

~~~

Tearing around the corner, Beneda comes to a halt and takes in a crazy scene. *What to do?* Pete down on the ground, a man tying his hands—*Cootuh's man?* The thin fellow works quickly, he warns Pete, "I ain't tryin' to hurt 'ya, son."

A man's down— at Marquetta's feet, and she's standing, grappling with another, this one, with a club.

Taking a calming breath, Beneda carefully aims into the man's back. *Thunk!* An instant later, with her arrow protruding from just left of a kidney, he staggers away from Marquetta's fists, a chance for her friend to reach down and grab up the club he's let fall.

In one more instant another man steps out from the library. This one, in a library guard's jacket, holding a staff. Scanning the group before him, he holds a lantern out. Another instant, and Zenobia's stepped out as well, dressed for bed, hair long down her back, she looks from the arrow Beneda's pointed at the men, to the men themselves.

What would Asante would do? Beneda remembers his words, 'make them come at us, one at a time.' Deciding, she shouts at Pete and Marquetta,
~~~

so they know she's there, and she steps over to Zenobia. Now there are two of them armed to defend the door and the tied up boy.

Marquetta turns her attention to Beneda for a second, then faces Cootuh, her club held high, and his two goons coming around the corner.

Cootuh! Silently Beneda curses the black turtle.

Putting a hand on Beneda's shoulder, Zenobia pulls herself up to her full height and speaks out. "Hear me. The authorities have been sent for." Beneda's liking the new, stronger Zenobia. "They will be here soon."

It's dim but Beneda observes Cootuh's calculating. In this moonlight his eyes give him away. Steadying her aim on him is easy in the moon's rays.

That reptilian glance travels to each person before the library. Her hand on the bow knows when he makes his decision. She breathes out again, once he directs the two closest to him. Pointing them to the wounded fighters, he gathers his people around him, stepping back out of range of the staff wielding librarian. Now six wait on each side in the Library's rear yard.

After a moment, making a mock bow, to the one with the staff, Zenobia, and Beneda with her bow, Cootuh herds his group, backward step by backward step, from the yard and back into the forest that edge into darkness.

19 Home Going - Soul

In the tavern, Jolan's stomach makes a small noise. He ignores it. Jolan thinks about the trip home with Marquetta. *Good theys take'n horses.* He grabs at cornbread, spying on Beneda, Pete, and the reporter sitting round the table. *Nah, nobody heard.*

The reporter lady, she asks, "How many were there." She writes in that little pad of hers.

Looking for them men in his mind, to his left, up high, Pete counts on his fingers, "Six."

"And you say this fellow, *Cootuh*, he's the leader?" *That mean turtle.* Jolan licks the butter from his fingertips. *Mebbe I tell her that for the story she gots goin'.*

Beneda makes a growly noise, "He spoke to me." *Miss Beneda, she hate 'im. If'n I sees him, I hate 'im too.*

More writing on the lady's pad of paper. "And you never saw Librarian Oliver?"

Marquetta sets down her spoon, and puts in her two cents, "He never come out last night." She *harumphs*. "After the sheriff come and take de report. After we sure the library folk lock up the building good, we leave."

"What time was that?"

Yawning wide, Pete, he tells her, "'bout three in

de mornin'."

"This is good information. I'm going to write this up and send it to my paper." Putting away her notes she gathers her bag, standing up. "Miss Marquetta, Jolan, have a good trip. Pete and Beneda, I will talk to you more."

Though Jolan keeps eating his cornbread, everyone else's attention follows the reporter woman as she leaves. Scratching her head, Marquetta ask, "'Neda, you think that Missus Chasseur might can help us? Writin' up a story 'bout a fight?"

"Don't know." Beneda doesn't bother with answering that, she be busy pokin' her breakfast he sees. "Jolan, you want this?" Smiling with joy, he reaches over for the extra food. While she tells her friend, "Maybe it helps, if more people know about the threat to our farms."

Pete's frowning. "An' if'n nobody care?"

"There's things to do." Beneda strokes Jolan's hair, ready to stand and get at them things. "Send Marquetta and Jolan home, get more farmers here, watch the library, send a letter to Asante, let him know he was right…"

Marquetta, she gots questions all her own, "Think he'll come back?"

Shaking her head, Beneda ignores that too. *All these here adults not saying what dey all wants to.* "We need to make a list of people we think can be spared. To come here to defend the library."

Pete scratches his chin. Like he has an itchy beard. He ain't got one a'tall. "You said harvest be mostly in. That should free up lotsa folk."

Bobbing her head, Beneda agrees, "Pete, write down who you think. Marquetta, can take our lists back when she goes." Putting her fist to her mouth, she ponders, then, "Recruit people, from all the farms, send them here." Jolan thinks, *I's a good recruiter. I run fast.*

"How many you want." Marquetta studies, like she trying to remember, in case numbers come at her.

Thinking some more, Beneda scratches her head, then, "We can't use everyone at once. Make a rotation. Send some right quick. Then send some each week." Pausing again. "Some go, some come. Each week."

Looking confused, Pete asks next, "What's you thinking?"

"We put a watch on." She reaches for Pete's hand. "We start at night. Then when we have more people, we stand watches all day and all night."

She nods. Jolan wiggles, another bit of bacon in his fist. *We's a team an' she's sure'a herself.*

~~~

Jolan likes this road. Nothing but trees, bushes and bird sounds, everywhere. The sweet smell of the Yellow Jessamine comes to him. He looks around for the birds he hears a'calling.

Marquetta, she don't care. She gets to fussing. "Stop daddling, Jolan."

"Can't help it. De horse won't go." His horse is moseying along, sniffing at the road flowers to the sides.

Her horse be moving away, Marquetta glances back and waves a fist at him, sets his legs to twitching. Finally, with some heels to its flank, the Marsh Tacky he sits gets back to walking forward slowly.

As Jolan clops up to Marquetta, their horses
~~~

move side by side. They turn their heads to a crashing noise in the trees to the right. Jolan opens his mouth, but Marquetta's hand goes up, stopping him.

Suddenly a man jumps onto the road. Out from behind those trees. Jolan jumps seeing a half eaten peach in one hand, pole in the other.

"Hah," he shouts. Both horses startle and skip sideways. Devil of a time keeping them from stomping on the fellow.

Shouting back, Marquetta berates him, "What you shout'n fer? Fool!"

Holding up that long pole, he makes to point it at Marquetta. "I 'spose to stop people comin' by."

Staring at him a moment, Marquetta puts her hand to her face, and commences to cryin'. *I cain't believe it*, Jolan's never seen her do that. The blubberin' an' wailin' comes on and on.

The man lowers his pole. Jolan is amazed. He's seen Marquetta knock down grown men. Seen her chase a bull across a field. But cryin', nah, he ain't never seen that.

That man, he say, "Aw, ma'am." A hand pats the air, "Now. Don't do dat."

Mumbling, Marquetta climbs down her Marsh Tacky. As the man reaches out to maybe help, Marquetta grabs him just that quick, knocks that pole right out his hand. *Wait'll I tell Pete!*

Struggling for a moment, the peach eater tries breaking free. Jolan reaches to grab her horses' lead. Marquetta, she's pushed a blade up against his neck. The man stops wriggling.

"Who you be?"

The fool, he stutters back, "Je—Jeremiah."

"Who set you on dis road?" She's holding the

blade tight against he Adam's apple, Jolan can feel it on his own neck she pressin' so hard.

"Ah…Ah, Cootuh." The fool's starting to shake all down to he toes. *Dat turtle!*

"*Dat* fool getting on my last nerve!" Marquetta seethes, in the next second come her nicest voice, she asks, "Do I have t' cut you, *Jeremiah*?"

"No…*ma'am!* No you don't! I be good."

Marquetta lets him loose, and he swarms in a puddle at her feet. "Jeremiah, you scat, now!" The knife shines in the sun, brighter than her smile. "Tell Cootuh, he better not mess wit us!"

~~~

Old Lady Harris sits on a high stool. She reading the letter from Beneda, that Marquetta done give her. Jolan's mouth waters. He can't stop watching the pot Missus Washington stirs. The steam brings great smells to him. He sits on the old rug beside Caleb. Beside Marquetta at the table, Old Willy drinks from a cup of tea.

"Missus Washington, how you fix your Frogmore stew?" Marquetta wonders.

Missus Washington, she give Marquetta a crooked look, "Girl, I do like my mama did." With one hand, she adds some shrimp. "M'Deah say, 'cordin' ta taste.'"

Laughing, Old Lady says, "Yo mama sure could cook." She points a scrawny hand at Marquetta. "I asked *her* de same." She tells her, "She give me the same answer."

Old Willy's face be lit up with a big smile. Caleb pokes Jolan's side, and gets a strong poke back. He tryin' to listen, Caleb he just want to play.
~~~

Missus Washington glances first to the boys then at the page in Old Lady's hand. "What my girl say?"

The finger still points to Marquetta. "Like she say, To send peoples to help keep watch at de library."

"Was she hurt?"

Shaking her head, Marquetta say, "No ma'am. Though Pete, he have a bump on he head."

Old Lady calls to Old Willy, "When that boy get back, I'ma send him to you to learn fighting." A frown crosses her face. "He mama was against it. Bless her soul. But, nows soon 'nough t' be learnt."

Missus Washington puts a finger in the stew, "What we gonna do?"

Old Lady looking to be thinking, she fanning herself with Beneda's letter. "We got to send help." She think some more, Jolan he waits, *might can be a message I can run wit*. "Then, we got to talk to more people. Old Willy, send a body t' Martin farm, have him come here. Time we alls chew on dis problem. And send a'nother t' the Brown place, see if young Turner come visit."

Old Willy, he looks to Missus Washington for permission, then nods. "Yas'um."

Old Lady brings that finger up, pointing at Marquetta again. "Girl, you go get Bessie, and some young folks. Beneda say we need a list fer who go to town. We folla' her lead."

Stopping her stirring, Missus Washington waves the wooden spoon at Old Willy. "Willy. You carry Tyrone. Go and see what my girl needs you do."

Bouncing up and down, Jolan wonders when the stew be ready.

Missus Washington casts her eye on him, she likes him when he der to help. "Child, get some bowls. 'Nough for everyone. This be ready soon."

Jolan bolts to the cabinet. Caleb following.

20 Port Wentworth - Heart

Biting into the cornbread, at her mother's table, Lakisha thinks how to tell her she wants to stay working at the library. Asante sitting across from her sips the tea mama handed him. Peanut sits by the door, stroking on Aza's fur, *the child cain't get enough of that pup*.

"Mister Scout, you should stay here." Mama uses a pleading tone, like she do at the cannery, for more shifts.

Setting down the cup, Asante shakes his head, not wanting to, but Lakisha knows he has to say, "I don't have business here, Missus Johnson."

Her face beaming, mama ain't hearin it. She starts a pitch. "This seems the month we finally vote out our crook of a sheriff." She keeps on, with nothing from the scout. "Sheriff Robbie. He need some capable helper to clean up the mess left by that waste of a badge we had."

"Thank you, ma'am, for thinking of me."

Nodding her pleasure, she turns to her daughter. "'Kisha, the cannery girls be asking if you be joining us this summer."

The time has come, Lakisha brings in a deep swallow of air then, "Mama. I want to go back an' work at the library. In Bluffton."

Half looking at her, mama busies herself with her cleaning towel, wiping the stove that already gleams. Finally, it comes out, “That’s what you want?”

Lakisha’s glad mama don’t seem mad, but then, *they's a guest sittin’ here*. “Oh yes, Mama. I do. I’m learnin’—*learning*.”

“Well … we gots to talk about it, at the end of summer. You need think about school again, hear?”

Lakisha’s whole face brightens with her joy. “Peanut can come and live with me at the library.”

Frowning, mama gives a sharp head shake. “Girl. You ain’t barely big enough to take care of yourself. How you gonna raise dis small boy?”

“But, Mama.” She argues, “There is a nice woman, name of Zenobia, she say she help me.”

“Humph! I’ll figure on it.”

Lakisha holds a piece of cornbread out to Peanut. “Peanut. You want to come live with me in Bluffton.”

Jumping up, the boy runs over and grabs the bread. Then breaking it in two he offers one piece to Aza and stuffs the bigger chunk in his mouth.

Nodding Peanut mumbles though his mouth full, “Yas’um.”

~~~

Even the crisp sea air hitting her face and nose can’t cheer Lakisha up. She regrets having to take Asante to the boat. Peanut walks with his hand on Aza’s back.

Few people are out on the early morning streets. “Wish you didn’t have to leave, Mister Asante.”

His kindly black face looks sad, then smiles gently, as he tells her, “I wish the same, little one.”

“I think Miss Beneda wishes you stay.” Lakisha
~~~

remembers the older girl's look, the last time.

Asante takes a deep breath, then tells the sky, “I miss her already.”

“Why can’t you stay?” she wonders.

“Older folks have responsibilities.” His face serious. “We must carry them out, even when we don’t want to.”

Lakisha tries jokes, “I don’t want to grow up.”

His big hand pats the top of her head. “Remember to honor your mother and your father.” Then waving over to the boy. “Raise the little one up to be an honorable man who will always stand for justice.”

Fighting not to show the tears, Lakisha nods. Looking away, looking ahead she sees the unwelcome masts of the clipper ship.

Peanut, he asks, “How long it be? To travel to…”

A shout comes from behind, "Scout!"

Turning, Lakisha’s used to seeing Asante’s hand move to the hilt of his sword, But Peanut, he jumps.

Stick— Seeing his big black shape makes Lakisha mad. Not scared anymore, she calls for Peanut, who runs to her side. Stick, he calling from behind his bodyguard. Two other big men with swords stand beside him.

Poking his head a little out, he call out like he the only one on the street, “I was sent word, I understand you are going home. These helpers are here to make sure you make your ship.”

Smiling, Asante drops his hand from his sword, taking a step toward the gangster. “It's a shame you came all this way, with nothing to do.” Seeing Asante move closer, Stick slides back a step, behind his big guard.

In a moment, he risks to come out once more. Reminds Lakisha of a scared turtle.

Stick licks his lips and tries sounding in charge, “Well. You ain't needed no more no ways.”

A cloud crosses the scout’s brow, he asks, “What are you on about?”

Stick smiles big now, feelin’ his oats, there’s more than just a taunt in his words. “The problem with the library is over. The businessmen, they’ve sent an armed group to deal with it. And the papers.”

Lakisha can’t tear her view from Asante’s expression. First an angry wave crosses his face, then nothing. *Like he frozen solid, a stone.*

That rock face turns to order Lakisha, “Take Peanut. Stand by that pole.” He points to the lamppost across the street.” Slowly.

She grabs the boy's hand and moves in the direction he’s pointed.

Asante’s voice follows them. “Aza. Guard!” She hears the swishing of the pup’s tail as it comes trotting. No words for the men behind her at all. She holds so tight to Peanut’s hand; the boy whines a bit.

Turning when she reaches the pole, Lakisha sees the scout pulling his sword loose and striding closer to Stick. The girl can read the terror gripping the bossman as he steps back.

Waving both arms, like a duck trying to take off, he stammers to the two strangers, “Stop him! Earn your pay!”

The one to the right wears leather armbands, stretching from each wrist to his shoulders.

Taking a step forward, he brags. “Never been defeated. Now I get a scout.”

Silently, cobra-like, Asante strikes forward. As

the leather clad one tries to swing, the scout twirls, stepping in a flash behind the brute, slashing at his leg. Instantly the big attacker is down, moaning and gripping his leg just above his bloodied heel.

The second man, with no leather, worked to get behind the scout. But he leaps back as Asante's sword takes a swing. A moment of wild flailing ends when the scout's sword hacks down hard on this man's arm, forcing him to drop his sword.

Without sparing a glance, Asante continues moving toward Stick, who's made it to the other side of the street now. The bodyguard, holds his arm, backpedaling, resisting Stick's urgent pushes in the scout's direction.

"Stand aside." Asante commands. "I have business with *him*!"

For a moment the guard weighs a decision. Looking from Asante to Stick. Then, dropping his club, he turns and runs for an alley without looking back.

Stick stares in amazement after his fleeing guard, then to the downed one still moaning in the street. Too fast for Lakisha to follow, the scout has sheathed his sword and reached Stick's side. Now Stick's neck is squeezed in a vice by Asante's hands.

"What is happening in Bluffton?" Asante asks slowly, like talking to Peanut.

Commencing to quivering in his fine boots, Stick stutters, "I—I don't know much. A—All I heard was the—" he chokes out, "T—they sent fighters to take the li—library."

"When?"

"Already done. All over."

Asante gives him a shake, "How do you know?"

Like an adult would a child.

"M—message said attack be yesterday."

The scout drops him, and Stick falls hard, bounces and groans. Asante turns, calling to Lakisha and Peanut, he walks away from the pier, in the opposite direction of the masted ship.

"Come Lakisha. There's things to straighten out…"

21 Business - Trickster

Cootuh tries to get comfortable on the blanket in the wagon's bed. The morning breeze is pushing the fog away. Another two hours of this. He's regretting being privileged to ride and recline at the same time.

"Aaron. Cain't you make this buckboard bounce a might less."

"Sorry, boss." Aaron looks recovered from being clobbered by that farmer woman. "only de new wagons have dem springs," he calls back to the two in the wagon."

"Dang." Looking at Barnabas, slouched in the buckboard with him, Cootuh curses to himself. "Worried about Barnabas' wound." That Miss Beneda is devilish with her bow.

"Cain't help it, Boss."

Cootuh thinks his walkers are lucky now. Froggy in front and Ben and Joel behind. He thinks on what his grandfather, the navy officer, who'd thrown him out when he was little, always said, 'Always know what's behind you, and in front'.

"We might be late to the meeting. But I don't care. My bottom can't survive much more jostling."

Licking his lips, and tightening his hold on the reins, Aaron asks, "Miss Octavia be there?"

Cutting a sharp look to Aaron's wide back, he

scolds. “Don’t worry yourself ’bout Miss Octavia. Think on drive’n good.”

Froggy raises an arm. Cootuh taps Aaron, so he sees. As the wagon stops, Cootuh glances to the two walking back of the wagon. Ben gots his sword ready. Joel holds his cudgel. Cootuh thinks how he’s good with a sword, his ownself. But, it’s important his men not think the boss has to do any fighting.

The bushes beside the road are disturbed as four dirty men walk on the road in front of the horses. These bandits look moderate well fed. Cootuh thinks they look more experienced than his men. *Time to talk good*.

“Hello friends. Glad to see you,” he calls from the wagon.

The leader shows his surprise. His leather vest is dusty. His sandals worn. He waves his big sword. “We here t’ rob you.”

“Ah. But I want to employ you.”

Showing confusion, the leader ignores that. “Give us your valuables. No one gets hurt.”

Shaking his head, keeping his smile big, Cootuh answers. “Can’t do that.” Then he holds up his hand. “But, I can do better.”

It takes a moment, but finally Cootuh hears, “What?”

Looking at the other three men before him. A young one with a bow, a scrawny one and one bigger man, Cootuh calls, “How would you all like a good meal? And some pay?”

The leader gives him a suspicious look. “Whatta we have’ta do?”

Cootuh nods, “Just what you’re doing now,” and pulls a pencil and scrap of paper from his pocket.

"Hold up travelers on the road to the Library, keep 'em from passing."

The lead bandit glances from member to member of his misbegotten crew. Studies their eyes for a bit then nods his consent.

"Okay, if'n you pay. We help."

Cootuh finishes a rough map with his pencil stub. Handing it over, he tells the bandit, "Here's a rough cabin, near the stream at Bluffton." Tapping at the picture he's drawn, "Meet me there. Tomorrow noon. Bring your men."

~~~

Cootuh walks across the clearing, just past Pritchardville, thinking, *This looks like a military camp*. One big white tent in the middle of the grounds, they've used it for an overnight bivouac. The tent's flap opens and falls with men walking in and out. *Changed a lot since a few days ago, bustlin' real nice now.*

Inside, Cootuh examines Octavia in her tight fitting jacket, with ribbons, and shiny metal buttons, looking like any army officer.

He worries, not seeing Malcolm.

"Where's Malcolm, ma'am?"

A hard look flashes across her face. "He's off to Bluffton. To fix *your* problem."

Hah! Malcolm's even less experienced in dealing with farmers than Octavia. *Serves him right.* "How many men he take with him?" He remembers Barnabas, with his wounds.

Looking down at the map on the table, she doesn't spare Cootuh a glance. "Five, Johnny and others."
~~~

A smile crosses his face. “Well, we better get ready to rescue him.”

That gets her attention. He stops smiling. He hedges, “The library will have strengthened their defenses.”

“Because of your failure,” she snaps.

Nodding in admission, he slips his hands in his pockets, a smaller target, he counters, “Yes, but they will be even harder to defeat. Miss.”

“If he can’t get the papers, Malcolm has orders to burn it down.”

Grimacing, in shock, *She would take that tact.* “But, we don’t want the libraries as enemies.”

Her elegant nails brush dust from her twill skirt. “What can they do? You said all their scouts are far away.”

Shaking his head, in exasperation, Cootuh can only take a deep breath.

“May I tell you a story?”

Skirt forgotten, she looks at him then. “Two years ago, Mustasfa Jones was robbing a store in New Orleans. Tussled with the local Librarian. Ended up, he cut off the man’s ear.”

Octavia’s expression remains bored. “So.”

“So, the New Orleans library set a scout on Mustasfa. Six months later she caught up with him up in Washington State and put Jones down. Four thousand kilometers across rivers, deserts, and snow covered mountains. For one man—because of an ear. When the man had a perfectly good one on the other side of his head.”

A frown crinkling her brows, Octavia nods. “I’ve given orders. No librarians are to be hurt.”

“Just books?” Cootuh shakes his head, giving up.

She smiles. *She's proud?* "Books and papers."

All that's left to Cootuh is exasperation. The big tent seems smaller all of a sudden. "Well, give the order." Trying to offer a respectful look. "If we leave quick, we can get to Bluffton by nightfall."

Octavia taps the map thoughtfully. "The morning's soon enough. Cook's caught some lovely bass at Stoney Creek. Promises quite a feast this evening. Get some sleep. Malcolm can take care of business, until then."

22 Library Watch - Warrior

On her side of the square, Beneda watches the mist drift through the trees. The morning sun begins to peek at the roof of the library. Struggling to keep her eyes open, she slumps on the bench. *Pete will soon be here.* Marshy smells come to her from the river, about a kilometer away. She needs sleep.

Sitting straighter and grabbing her bow with a stiffer grip, she reacts to the library's front door opening. Then, relaxes seeing Zenobia step out. The woman in her typical brightly colored robe leads a man over to where Beneda sits watch.

Giving a little head bow, she waves at the young man beside her. "Librarian Lincoln has sent Preston to help us." *Ah, from Beaufort.*

Tiredly, rubbing at her sore arm, Beneda returns the smile, wishing they'd sent more than a single librarian. "Any other help coming?" Beneda feels Zenobia looks fresh and awake. And it crosses her mind, she'd love a bath and ten hours of sleep.

With a sad quirk to her lips, Zenobia shakes her head, she does add, "Librarian Lincoln's sent for a scout. But doesn't know when she will arrive, a pigeon we received says she is in Virginia."

The word *scout* takes Beneda's mind drifting down a dark path. Shaking her head to drive the confused thoughts away, she merely says, “Oh.”

Zenobia points back to the Library’s huge windows, the fog just clearing under the casements. “The Librarian has finally given permission to fortify our defense. We’ll do all the wings. We’ll start boarding up all the ground floor windows, today.”

That wakes Beneda some. “I’m expecting more help soon.”

Zenobia approves this news. Nodding to Preston, and replying vigorously, “Wonderful news!” and then, in a lowered tone, “The sheriff’s not helping.” She mentions this with a twist to her lips; Beneda can see she’s probably caught in a difficult situation, and not just being circumspect with Preston here.

Beneda thinks how little help she got with her kidnapping, and the attack the other night. “Riley has been useless, so far…” Preston just stands there. Nothing to add.

Slipping her hands into her sleeves seems to be an end to that line of talk, because Zenobia tries with something positive, “He says he hasn’t enough men to help with a problem like this. Says he sent to the capital for armed marshals.”

At this Preston shows interest, “How many people do you think it would take to defend your library?”

Zenobia’s gaze wanders to her left, studying those wide windows, and Beneda likes that Zenobia offers, “The books say, it all depends. How skilled our people are.”

Preston adds, “And, how skilled the enemy is.”

“My people aren’t skilled fighters, we farm.”

Looking like he's reading a book. “They say we should try to have twice as many. According to the old books about war."

Beneda stares at her bow, thinking about all the names Pete and she had come up with to call to action. "I will send for more." She's worried that her people might get hurt over this. But, M'Deah would say, *no price is too high*.

Pointing down the street, Zenobia answers, "Looks like Pete's coming." She touches Preston's arm. "Let's go. We have window boarding to organize."

Giving her a smile, Beneda waves and thinks, what comes *next*?

~~~

By ten that morning, no sun reflects off the Library's front façade. Beneda tries ignoring Pete staring at her from the opposite side of the bench. *Maybe something to distract him?*

"Zenobia set you to use a hammer I see, boarding up the windows today on the north side."

Glancing over, she sees his nod, and smiles as he parrots: "She says they are determined to resist another attack." *Does he mean he's worried about me?* He schools her, "It's dangerous what we are doing."

"Yeah. But, we have to preserve the farms." She examines his eyes; *does he understand what this really means?* "It is more important than my life, or yours, Pete. This is about the future of our people."

Pete seems unsure how to react, and suddenly she recognized more of the boy than the man in him. He tries, says, "I know. But…"

Beneda's thinking he can't say what he means. "Yes?"
~~~

Looking like he's struggling, expressions pass on his face, like disturbed water until he's decided, "Beneda—"

She waits, giving him time. His eyes go down to his pants pocket. Digging there, like a hungry person searching for food, he pulls out a small box. His face glows, like he's won a prize.

Beneda's eyes can't move from the object in Pete's hand. She watches like it's a snake. "What's that?"

"I…It for you." He scoots closer and reaches it over. For the longest time, her hand won't move. Finally, she accepts the tiny black box, wary at the lightness of it in her hand.

Gazing into his eyes, she tries to decide what to do with the closed offering. What will it mean if she opens it? His eyes are mostly steady, focused on hers. She swallows, but her throat is too dry. Pete's pleading look convinces her to risk seeing what is inside.

Opening the box reveals a set of earrings. Little black pearls. *Where in the world could he have gotten them?*

Biting her lip, Beneda struggles with what to say. She's so worried, tired, and sleepy. *How do I do this?*

"Pete, thank you." Pausing. "But…I can't accept these. We know each other too well, what would folks say? We nearly kin."

His face falls. *Upset, of course.* She closes the box and holds it up to him. *What can save this? I need him. We need him.*

Pete doesn't move for a minute. At last, his hand reaches for it.

She has to keep him here. "Pete." His eyes find

hers. He looks like a puppy. “I need you. Please help me. We—*this*—is more important.”

His face changes. Yes. “Okay, Beneda. You know you can count on me.”

“Yes, Pete. I know.”

~~~

A gentle hand wakes Beneda. Rubbing her eyes, she takes in the library and trees. *Still on the bench*. If she rubbed a lamp and had a genie, she’d wish for a soft warm bed and clean clothes. She can’t be smelling too good either. Pete points to the road, the sun’s heading down. Beneda spies two riders hitching their horses.

Old Willy, and Tyrone.

“Finally.” Pete’s voice sounds as tired as she feels.

Approaching, the two men both lift their hats to her. Willy gets right to it. “Miss Beneda. We here. What you need us do?”

Returning a weary smile, Beneda looks them over. “Thanks Willy. And thank you too, Tyrone.” She hesitates, this will be harsh. Silently, a curse crosses her mind for the sheriff. Deciding between the two farmers, she settles her eyes on Tyrone. “I’m sorry Tyrone. You have to ride back.”

Old Willy gives her a glance that’s just shy of a rebuke. *Better explain*. “The library has no fighters. We all have to defend this place.”

With practiced eyes, Willy looks over the building, around at the trees. “Ma’am, I don’t like des ground. Be better to move the papers to someplace like de jail. We can better defend.”

Shaking her head. “I know you’re right. But
~~~

Librarian Oliver won't let us."

Looking doubtful, Old Willy again looks at the building, wooden boards covering the lower windows. He walks to the nearest side. At his tired expression, as he returns, she feels bad.

Turning to Tyrone, Old Willy repeats her orders, and then some. "Tyrone, take both horses. Go back, have them send as many people as they can. Twenty, if'n they can."

23 Library - Heart

They've come up from the river, on the path through the trees, which leads up to the Library's back façade. Asante stops and crouches down quickly. Lakisha has no idea why he's stopped and her eyes go to Aza who is still, with his ears tilted forward.

In a low voice, Asante orders, "Hold. There're men there." He points ahead into the trees.

In the direction where the scout and Aza are peering, Lakisha spies several men standing around the beginning of a campfire. She wonders if they made it here from Port Wentworth? The Scout counts off the ones in plain view, he stops at six. Through the branches and scrub brush ringing the Library's back grounds, she sees that three have weapons out, they seem to be arguing. One man is bandaging the arm of another, a meter away from the others.

From his crouched position, Asante wiggles his finger past them. She spots the library wall. A couple of meters beyond these half dozen strangers.

Moving his head close to hers, he whispers, "Think you can sneak past them?" Still hidden in the trees, she judges the open space, and the distance she's got to move around these fellows, here in the trees, and on to the Library's back door.

Nodding vigorously, she moves her lips, forming,

'yes.'

Pointing to the left, softly Asante whispers, "Sneak through the bushes. If you need to abandon the library, lead the library staff to me."

She gets ready to move. His hand grips her shoulder.

"You remember the inn the farmers stay at?" Lakisha thinks of the night when she slept beside Aza, in Beneda's room. "They'll be in town by now. Let them know that inside." Then, he pushes Lakisha gently toward those thicker bushes.

"Go slowly." Asante's soft voice ordering, "Aza, stay."

Creeping around the men and their fire, Lakisha stays low, down away from sight. The group of men have no idea she's there.

It seems to take forever to get close to the building. Two men stand beside the back door. One is Owen the library guard, holding his staff. The other is the young farmer, a friend of Beneda. Running the last meter, she makes the door in steps she counts in her head.

"Lakisha!" Owen calls out.

She squeaks back, "Owen."

Pressing her hands against the door, she looks back into the fading light filtering through the trees. *Where's Asante*. Looking back, she can make out wisps of smoke from the men's siege fire.

The farmer lad asks, "How'd you get here?"

"Asante." Waving toward the trees. "He out there."

Owen lowers his voice, "Did you see attackers?"

Shaking with worry, she answers, "Six, we count. One look injured, so five I say."

"Pete did that. Let's go in. Bolt this door. Less to deal with."

Lakisha agrees, outside is too dangerous.

Stepping in the doorway, Zenobia stands with knitted brows. The night guard, Abe, sits holding a bloody cloth to his arm. She runs to him, and he smiles, saying, "Hey there!" Beside Zenobia stands another man. Preston, from Beaufort, Lakisha remembers his vest.

Touching Owen's shoulder, Zenobia asks, "How many?"

Sparing a glance to Lakisha, he says, "Five. With swords. They've gone nearly into the woods."

Zenobia embraces Lakisha. "You're back." Her eyes scan the girl from top to bottom. "Asante?"

Nervously watching the door, Lakisha answers, "In the woods, too."

A firm nod, and Zenobia's eyes find Pete. "Pete, you and Owen stand guard at this door. Barricade it."

Touching Zenobia's hand, Lakisha asks, "Is cook here?"

With a head shake. "No. I sent her home."

Looking at the others in the flickering lamp light, Lakisha decides. "I will make sandwiches. Oh! And also the farmers should be on their way, Ma'am."

Smiling, Zenobia pats her back. "Preston, help Lakisha. And take Abe with you."

Preston helps Abe up and the pair follows Lakisha down the hallway.

~~~

After taking food to Pete and Owen, and returning to the dining room, Lakisha joins Preston and Abe at the table.
~~~

Watching Preston re-bandaging the guard's arm, Lakisha pays attention to the man from Beaufort for the first time. She sees the light brown of his face has freckles.

Abe winces. "Ouch."

Clanking sounds accompany Zenobia's entrance. Lakisha sees she carries a helmet, and heavy clothing.

"Lakisha. Help with this."

Stepping over, Lakisha helps pile the things on a chair. Looking between it and Zenobia, she wonders what's going on.

Giving her a somber look, Zenobia declares, "I have a serious job for you."

Eagerly, Lakisha stands taller. "Yas'um."

"Those men out there have started loosing fire arrows onto our roof."

Lakisha hadn't noticed, hadn't once looked out any window since making the library's back door. Now she's worried.

The Librarian shrugs, giving a small smile, and assures her, "They're probably wasting their arrows. The roof is mostly tile." Her finger stabs the air. "But, there are a few spots up there that are not protected."

"What I need do?" Lakisha wants something, anything, to do to help. Though both men with her remain silent.

"Don this armor. You'll fit were others can't. Go on the roof. With buckets of sand, you can extinguish the arrows."

Lakisha's eyes return to the pile on the chair. Picking up the helmet, she tries it on. It fits pretty good. A chuckling sound draws her eyes to Abe. He smiles fit to bust. She's glad Preston has a serious look on his face, when he offers, "I'll carry up sand buckets, will four do?

"Yes. Do nicely." Zenobia picks up another piece. "This is the breastplate." As she helps Lakisha into it, it seems to fit like it's made for her. "We had this Japanese armor in the basement. I thought the size was about right."

Feeling very bulky Lakisha waddles like a duck as Zenobia moves to the door.

She tells Preston, "I have a bucket of sand at the stairs. We'll get the others to you shortly." Zenobia follows Lakisha, adding, "Thank you for doing this."

Lakisha notices Librarian Oliver carrying luggage, coming toward them. She has to stop and scoot to the wall.

Zenobia doesn't move. The man has to stop. "Librarian. Going somewhere?" *Her voice sounds like mama's.*

His bags shift in his hands, he blusters, "I'm making a visit to the Hilton Head Branch." When she doesn't move, he continues. "They have been asking me to come. So I want to help them."

Zenobia moves to the side, slowly. "Pleasant journey." Her back turns on the Librarian and the boarded windows.

Lakisha thinks, *Please Lord, I don't never want t' ever hear tha' tone pointed to me.*

Librarian Oliver frowns at her, instead of at Zenobia, as he scurries to the front door. "Make sure my library doesn't burn down while I'm gone."

24 Prelude - Warrior

A smile creases Beneda's face as Tyrone rides up with another young man beside him. *New farmers!*

This new man brings a staff.

"Miss Beneda." Tyrone bends a bit towards Old Willy, then greets her, then, "Yo mama say more be coming. Most likely tomorra. This be Eli, from Martin's farm."

"Good, Tyrone." She nods to the other. "Welcome Eli."

"Miss Beneda."

From out of the trees a few meters away, a figure walks toward the four who stand smiling and nodding. Beneda sees it's the reporter from Beaufort. Missus Chasseur. *Why she come that way, instead of out on the road*?

From the shade of a lone tree, Missus Chasseur frowns at the three men then turns the frown on Beneda. With a gloved finger she points, her eyes sparkle, but not with fear at all, "Around back. Men are attacking." She now eyes each of the men as if already writing in her mind.

At this report Beneda's eyes whip to Old Willy. Eli makes a low sharp noise in his throat and pulls the men's horses off to the stanchion, out of the way. Old Willy, he grabs up his club.

"How many?" Beneda asks.

The reporter shakes her head. "I don't know. Maybe a handful, I managed a count of four, maybe five, but I was in the trees. There may be others." She tilts her head back to the stand of trees she's come from, "I think I saw that library scout, Asante. Keeping an eye on their movement."

Beneda's lungs feel like the air's been stolen from her. She forces herself to stop and think. *Defend the front door? Find out what's happening at the back?* Looks again to Old Willy, pleading in her eyes, a hand on his arm, she doesn't need to speak. *And Asante?*

"I take Eli and Tyrone." He assures her. "We see what's happenin'."

"Thank you Willy."

As the three men make their way around the side of the building, Missus Chasseur brushes off the bench and sits, opens her reticule, drawing out her notebook and pencil.

"It's becoming dangerous around here, Beneda." She taps at the notebook. Beneda agrees, staring at the building. *Can it survive a siege? So many wings, so many windows to breech?*

Taking another deep breath and checking her bow is ready, she wrestles all the questions in her mind, finally asking, "You saw Asante, Missus Chasseur?"

"Please, call me Savannah." She examines her gloves, dusty now from the bench. "I think so. There *were* men with swords. I was trying to stay out of sight."

"I hope he *is* here." Beneda says, trying not to stutter.

The reporter looks closely at Beneda's face,

sympathy dawns in her eyes for a second. “He’s rather good looking, that scout.”

Beneda checks her bow again. “Librarian Oliver left.” At Savannah’s sneer, she adds, “Just a few minutes ago, with his bags.”

Tap-tap-tap goes that pencil. “Well, Librarian Oliver is going to have some hard questions after this is over.” Then touching Beneda’s hand, Savannah changes her tone. “I’m going to help. I’ve sent for my husband; he’ll find a way to send a medical person.”

“Thank you Savannah.” Beneda stares at the library building, and tightens the grip on her bow. “I wish I knew what the future holds.”

~~~

As minutes tick by, Beneda sits beside the reporter, anxiously waiting to hear from Willy about what’s happening behind the library. No noise travels from back there. Perhaps… She pictures the buildings layout from above, as if seeing a map, the thick center of the Library, the two wings, less wide, jutting out left and right. Making a flattened cross shape for a footprint. Again she worries, *So many wings, so many windows*

The library’s door opens. Zenobia looks around and relaxes, only seeing the women on the bench. Beneda notices a large book under her arm as she hurries to them.

“Beneda…, Savannah.” She greets them. “Glad it’s quiet on this side.”

Beneda quickly blurts. “There *is* trouble back there? Asante might be there— in the woods.”

Slowly nodding Zenobia says. “Yes, Lakisha is here. She’s told me, with his dog.”
~~~

Beneda releases a breath she didn't know she was holding. "Good."

Glad her news has made the ladies smile, she looks down to the book then to Beneda, Zenobia says. "Here. If anything terrible happens, I wanted you and your people to have this."

Taking the thick book into her hands, Beneda feels the rough old cover binding, it must weigh two kilos or more. "What is this?"

"A record of local Gullah history. It mentions your family name." Zenobia says, softly.

Beneda finds it difficult to speak, for some reason, the book now seems to weigh more. "Thank you."

At that moment, the three women startle back; an arrow comes flying over the library's roof. *An archer of some worth must be back there.* Rising to her feet, Beneda judges the arc of its flight. *It'll miss us*. Her calculation is correct, it falls short, less than a meter to their left. Savannah trots over to try stamping it out with her buttoned up shoes.

One bounce and it skitters along the stones, stopping at the edge of the short grass, where it smokes as it continues burning. Quickly stepping past the reporter, Zenobia lifts her robe and calmly stomps on the flaming tip.

Savannah's eyes are round and wide watching her.

With a wave toward the building, where the arrow's come from, Zenobia informs them, "Yes, they're trying to burn the library." She seems surprisingly unruffled.

Excitedly, Beneda points at the houses a block over, behind the women. "What about your neighbors?"

Zenobia, perhaps noticing for the first time people walking about their business, looks down the street. "Should we warn them?"

Beneda settles her gaze at the closest building. *Alarm others? Have more deaths on her hands?* "Perhaps just the sheriff, or his deputy need to know." The two-story structure is more than a hundred meters away. "Isn't that a school?"

Nodding, Zenobia tells her, "Elementary students. I've talked there. About forty children."

Beneda's determined to act to move them out of danger's way. "I'll go. We've got to send them all home."

Zenobia nods at that idea. "I'd forgotten. I did send the cook home, with instructions to get word of our plight to Sheriff Riley."

Savannah *harumphs*. She reaches for Beneda's arm as she digs in her handbag. Pulling a small face mirror out, she hands it over. "Beneda. I accompanied an army raid on an illegal armory last year. They'd use small mirrors to look around corners. Before moving."

"Yes. Thanks, Savannah."

~~~

Through the school door, Beneda searches for someone in authority. Seeing a young man at a desk, she hurries over.

"There is fighting at the library. A siege. The children here must evacuate!"

He puts a hand to his chest and blurts, "Yes Ma'am! I'll tell the class down here. There's another upstairs." He points to the stairway. *Good man.*
~~~

"I'll get them." She shouts as she runs to the stairs, "Use the back door. Lead them still farther away from the library."

Taking the steps two at a time she reaches the top floor in moments. As she looks for the right room, she tries to think what a fight between her farmers and Cootuh's thugs will mean for the locals. *How can I keep them from harm?*

She hears laughter from one room along the hall. And tells herself, *Cootuh doesn't want to hurt people.'* But, still she worries.

Her stomach makes a growling noise, loud in the empty hallway. More than a day since the last real meal. Stopping to listen, now she hears children's voices.

Following the sounds, she reaches a closed door. Twenty young faces greet her after she pulls it open. Some children have crackers in their hands. Her stomach growls again. She gestures the teacher over.

As the young woman reaches her, Beneda whispers.

Taking in the teacher's shock, she continues, "Lead your students out the back door. I'll follow behind. Your man downstairs is doing the same."

Taking a breath and standing tall, the woman nods to Beneda, turns, clapping her hands, she announces. "Children. Stand and pick up your bags. We are going to have a fire drill." As the noise level rises, she speaks louder, "Alicia you are front of the line. Doug, you are at the end. Let's go." She claps her hands smartly.

Opening the door wide, Beneda and the teacher step out of the room, as the children's voices rise with questions.

"Quiet! Join hands with the one behind you and in front." She waits until a long twisty snake has formed. "Alicia, everyone, start."

The line dances down the hallway. Beneda falls in behind the little boy, Doug.

Following the group down the stairs, she tries to look in every direction.

At back door, she waves to Doug and the teacher at the front of the line. Closing the door, she listens in the quiet. *Sounds empty.*

Making her way to the front door, she takes out Savannah's mirror, *Thank goodness for small favors, and vain women.* Cracking open the door, sounds come to her from outside, men walking in front of the school. *Could be the sheriff?* Crouching down, she angles the mirror to see out the door's edge besides the doorframe. *No such luck.* She counts seven, but there may be more.

Cootuh! A shiver goes down her back seeing him motion, calling for the others to stop.

His voice comes to her, "There's the library. We'll station some to guard the front. Then look for Malcolm in back."

Beneda tries to keep from shaking as the group marches off. On the floor she crawls to the front window, focuses her eye on the library's façade in the distance. Luckily, no sign of Savannah and Zenobia.

What to do?

From her spying spot, she waits a few minutes, but sees only two of Cootuh's men in front of the library. One holds a sword, the other paces with a thick club on his shoulder. Rising to her feet, she determines her path. It hits her for a moment, she is carrying Zenobia's valuable book.

Throwing open the door, she steps out and unslings her bow and starts running. It's easier than she expects. Fear has left her. No need for worrying

Loosing an arrow when close enough, she aims for the swordsman first. *A hit!* But as the men run for safety to the side of the building, all her remaining tries miss their mark.

Halting, breathing heavy, nocking another, she looks around. It's quiet. Except she sees Savannah and Zenobia stepping out the trees to the side. Their mouths open.

"My!" Zenobia exclaims, her fine shoes bouncing on the stone hard ground as she runs close. Beneda grips the bow, her mouth dry, listening for attackers. "Remind me not to offend you."

Shaking her head, Savannah says, "Yeah. And remind me I want to sit down with you when all this is over, Beneda." The reporter pulls out her pad and pencil, scribbling.

Still looking around for danger, Beneda asks, "Where'd they go?"

Zenobia points right, sure of herself. "Headed around back."

Looking that way, the women are surprised by sounds from the far side of the building.

Cracking noises of branches announces Willy leading Eli around the corner.

Beneda swivels her bow and looks behind him. "Where's Tyrone?" she asks, as soon a Willy is close enough.

Willy pats a hand down. "Set him on a task. He be here in a lil' bit. Miss Zenobia." Willy looks to the librarian. "Your back door seem very solid."

Beneda's attention goes to the bundle of sticks

both Willy and Eli carry.

Nodding, she answers, “Yes. Heavy metal, and Pete and Owen have it barricaded it from the inside.”

“Good.” He says, “And it would take monkeys to get to the little windows back there.”

Beneda can’t wait any longer, she’s worried about what Cootuh will do next. “What are those for?”

Willy gives her a chilly smile. “We funnel them here to the front. I gots some surprises for them.” He sits and starts whittling a sharp point on the first stick, Beneda hadn’t known about this skill. “I learned some things when a little boy.” He tells the Librarian. Then to Beneda, “Beside your M’Deah, defending the farms.”

25 Library Fire - Trickster

Sweat pours down Cootuh's neck as he tramps through the trees. Seven men remain with him with two more deployed at the front. A burnt grassy smell assails his nostrils as he steps around the corner.

"Jeremiah, go watch behind us. I don't like surprises."

No-see-ums buzz around his head. Approaching a crackling fire, Cootuh sees Malcolm yelling directions at a young bowman.

Malcolm points to the roof and screams, "Hit 'er!"

Looking up, Cootuh's angle doesn't allow him to see anyone above. Motioning his men to spread out behind, he moves to Malcolm. Several men sit on the ground fashioning crude arrows for the bowman.

Cootuh observes a look on Malcolm's face, never before directed at him. Malcolm seems almost relieved to find Cootuh's arrived.

"Cootuh! Good. You got another bowman?"

With a quick nod, Cootuh yells over to Nick, the young, recruited highwayman.

Wordlessly, Malcolm directs the boy to join the other bowman. And turns back to Cootuh, explaining, "Trying to burn the building." *Don't look like they're having much luck.* "Roof's mostly tile or stone. And some girl's up there with a damn bucket of water or something."

Again, Cootuh examines the roof and back wall they're meant to breech. From his vantage point, the roof appears mostly flat. He offers, "What about the back door?"

"Metal. Seems solid," Malcolm complains.

Cootuh thinks, but doesn't say aloud, *Damnit you fool, we need to end this quick*. "Wasn't the front door wood? If we had a battering ram—"

Shaking his head, Malcolm cuts that off, "—sent two off looking for a down'd log. Don't have no heavy axes." With a frown at the trees all around them. All looking healthy and thick. Cootuh waves over Sam, the highway bandits' leader.

"Sam, get a group to search for something we can use as a battering ram on the door." Pausing, he thinks. "Long, but solid. Put two men on finding a smaller tree and work on it with our two hand axes" Malcolm's ears turn a satisfying red. So Cootuh pokes deeper, "we can use a back up. Right Mister Malcolm?"

With a nod, the bandit leader gathers some of the men to him, and barks out Cootuh's orders.

"When will Octavia be here?" Malcolm seems as nervous as Cootuh feels. *Wants to succeed before she arrives?*

"Maybe by tonight." Cootuh's reply comes with a silly smile. "She's moving the whole camp. Like a huge circus."

Malcolm smiles too, before catching himself and wiping his grin away.

"Do we know where the papers are? When we get in? Which room to head for?"

Luckily for Cootuh he's got his library spy; he nods. "Yep. In a safe, in the Librarian's office. I don't have the combination. But, it's small, we should be able to cart it away."

Malcolm opens his mouth, but they're distracted by sounds of crashing and two men tear round the southern corner. Cootuh recognizes the ones he left to guard the front door, and curses all libraries near and far.

One, Kevin, stumbles, with an arrow shaft in his arm. "What happened?" Cootuh shouts.

"Some crazy woman attacked us!" Kevin wails, tripping to a stop.

Beneda! Damn her.

Malcolm's mouth opens, wide as his eyes at that. "One *woman*?"

The other runner looks sheepish, letting Kevin speak. "She charged us, too many arrows!"

Cootuh spits. "Where's your sword?"

Kevin frantically points to the shaft coming from his arm.

"What should we do?" Malcolm's turned back to Cootuh, ignoring the two runners.

Scanning the area around the fire, the trees beyond. The solidness of the Library itself. Cootuh takes a rough count. "We have to move fast. Before she gets more people." With a loud shout, "Everybody! Drop what you're doing. Form up!"

"Kevin. Stay and tend the fire. Malcolm take four men around the far left side. I'll go with the other three." At Malcolm's nod, Cootuh counts off the men. Waiting until Malcolm moves, he orders, "Count to twenty when you see me. Then attack."

Cootuh leads his small group to the right. "Let's

take this blessed building."

26 Farmers - Soul

The sun sits on the treetops now, and Jolan's glad the farmers have finally arrived at Bluffton. Kicking up dust, with the shuffling of so many feet. Walking beside Caleb, both boys carry the heavy bundles assigned to them, *precious bundles*, Missus Washington has lectured. After walking all day, in a few minutes they should reach the library, to help Beneda.

"Smoke be risin' from near the library." Marquetta exclaims.

"This ain't good," mutters Old Lady Harris. And behind, from the group, noises of concern rise. "We gots to find out what's happening."

Jolan watches as she casts her eyes over the farmers around her on the road. Finally, she settles on him.

"Jolan. Child, drop yo pack. Run, go find Beneda. Ask what she want us to do." She holds a hand out as he drops the bundle. "Be careful. They might be danger."

Nodding, he trots off. *Ain't afraid. Ain't afraid,* echoes with each running step.

Jolan passes scared people on the street. Everyone stays away from where the fire's risen. In minutes he can see the library. *Ain't burnin'*. But smoke rises from behind the tile roof.

The smell reaches him, but everything is quiet. No bird sounds or anything. Men crouch near the library's front door. Jolan sees one jump back as an arrow slams into the door, near him. That one has a huge head of hair, looks strong.

He remembers Beneda's arrow scaring a bear near home. Turning to see where the arrow's flew from, he sees Beneda, bent low against the school steps. Trotting over, he tries to stay hidden in bushes.

Pete, with a sword in his hand sees him. "Jolan!"

Where'd he get a sword? Pete's got a bandaged hand though, *must be a good sharp one,* he thinks.

"Pete! Where you get dat?"

Pete's ignoring that. "Where everybody else?"

That reminds Jolan what Old Lady said. "They's down the road, 'bout a minute 'er two behind. I ran. I gots to tell'em what to do."

"Beneda. Where you want the folks with Jolan?"

Beneda gots her arrow pointed across to the library. Jolan don't see no more in her quiver, or nowhere.

Without looking over, she calls out. "Have'em come here. They can set up in the school."

Jolan don't wait. He turns and sneaks back through the bushes. Once they all arrive, he and Caleb, they can ditch they heavy packs. *Mebbe go find Beneda's arrows for her.*

Running straight up to Old Lady, he blurts, "Beneda and Pete, they across from de library at de school. She say come on up. They's bushes to hide in der." He takes a breath, remembering her arrow almost hitting the strong man. "She outta arrows."

Old Lady grabs at his shoulder. “Jolan. You done good. Caleb. Hurry here.” Caleb comes over with one pack. “Martin, give Jolan he pack.”

“Yas’um.” Mister Martin lowers Jolan pack back to him. *Aw, now, how I gonna run fast with dis?*

“Jolan, you and Caleb hurry de packs of arrows to Beneda.”

“Yas’um!”

Then she waves at Martin. “Martin… Marquetta, you go with the lil’ ones.”

Jolan eyes Caleb and they hurry off, as fast as they can, with the heavy packs. Their bare feet slap the ground. Jolan thinks it funny how even with the packs, they soon leave Mister Martin and Miss Marquetta behind.

Beneda kneels, watches, and grips her useless bow when the boys reach her. Her bow across her knee, she gives them a sad look. Jolan assures her, “They’s comin’.”

Bouncing with energy again. *Now I can do somefin!* Stopping right in front of Beneda, he sets his pack on the ground.

“Caleb and I, we broughts you help’.” She squats and starts unwrapping. Caleb steps up and lowers his pack, too. *Now, she look like the girl dey know.*

With a smile, Beneda says. “Thanks.” *She tired, hope her arm still awake.*

Caleb pipes up. “Yo mama an’ Old Lady gots arrows. Alla the farms. For you. De farmers, dey be here direc’ly.”

She done already nocked one and aims at the library. Pete gathers the boys, moving them back.

“Let Beneda work.”

The two adults quickly join them behind Beneda,

as she sights, loosing one more before she stops to embrace Marquetta.

In minutes, the larger group starts streaming through the trees and bushes to gather, low around them. No one making much of a sound. Eyes wide.

Lowering her bow as the crowd grows behind her, Jolan sees tears coming down Beneda's cheeks when her mama lays a hand on her shoulder. *Why she upset? We brung arrows?*

"You're here." Sounds raspy, Jolan looks away as something gets in his eye, too.

"Yeah, girl. We brought twenty people, counting lil ones." Marquetta whispers low, waves at Jolan and Caleb, proudly standing beside the bundles of arrows. "Asante here?"

Taken a long time to answer, Beneda finally says, "Yes." She points to the library. "Somewhere over there."

Old Lady crabwalks slowly, nearly on her knees, she moves closer. "You speak to the scout, girl?"

Shaking her head, and wiping her eyes, Beneda tells her, "Ain't seen him yet."

Marquetta grips her shoulder. "Asante be looking for you, fore the day's done." She sounds certain.

Giving a little smile, Beneda says, "I hope he finds Old Willy, too. I expect he's causing trouble round back."

Old Lady waves Mister Martin, and Young Mister Turner over. Young Mister Turner limps over with his crutch.

Old Lady asks, "Beneda, how many they got?"

Rubbing her jaw. "I saw about ten. Savannah, you saw about five earlier?" Speaking to the well-dressed woman, that Missus Chasseur, gets a nod.

Mister Martin speaks, "What should we do?"

Beneda looks around at the farmers. "I'm going upstairs. I can see better and my bow will have better range." Then to Young Mister Turner, "Organize the people to defend this area. We need something like a small camp here, out of range. You can set up to cook in the school. They's running water. Pots and stuff."

Old Lady points to the packs with a stern look at Caleb and Jolan. *Aw, not again!* They tote the arrows and follow Beneda into the building. Miss Marquetta, Pete, Martin and Old Lady come too, the others stay behind, moving where Young Mister Turner points. *Glad to be settin' they packs down from the sounda it.*

Now, Jolan's getting tired. He an' Caleb drag behind the others, going no faster up the stairs than Old Lady.

~~~

Looking out the window, Beneda takes a moment to aim, then releases. They all standing in a school classroom. Little chairs and desks spread around the room. A map of America's forty-nine states drawn on the chalkboard.

The clicking of paws announces a dog.

"Aza!" Caleb shouts and runs over to hug the pup. The scout, Asante, comes through next pushing a man whose hands are tied, *Golly*, Jolan thinks, *a prisoner!*

The scout pushes the trussed man in Pete's direction and quickly moves to Beneda. She lowers her bow and the two embrace. *Ew, don't need t' see that!* Jolan glances back to Pete, he looks angry. Like he wants to run his sword through the roped man.

A gasp pulls his eyes over to Beneda's mama.
~~~

She surprised. But, slowly her face turns into a smile.

"Asante. You're safe." Her hands run along his arms. *What she check'n for?* "Did you see Old Willy?"

Patting her shoulder gently, the scout says, "Yes. He and two others, planting traps on the right side of the building."

Beneda lets out a loud breath. "Thank you. I worried so."

Old Lady interrupts, she waves her hand to the window. "How we stop em!"

"I been keeping them away from the big front door with a shot now and then." Beneda answers, "They drug up a big log, trying to get that door open. I was afraid they'd rush us soon."

The reporter lady adds, "You need a large armed force to come and arrest them."

"What about the army base on Parris Island?" Missus Washington turns to the Scout, a question in her eyes.

At that Old Lady raises her crooked hand, "Martin. Ain't your girl married to one o' them army commanders."

"My Carrie, she married to Captain Porter. He command a pike company."

The reporter has her notebook out. "Perhaps, you should go with a request for help."

Nodding, Martin says, "Yes, Ma'am. I ride there. What I need?"

Old Lady sits on one of the little chairs, and speaks up to those circled around her, "De mos' help be a letter from de Librarian."

Shaking her head, Beneda breaks her news, "Librarian Oliver is on his way to Hilton Head

Island."

With a smile, the scout lays a hand on Old Lady's palm, "Zenobia may be able to give you the letter you need."

Old Lady exchanges a look with Beneda and her mama, then she smiles, Jolan reads in those eyes, *We womens, we get things done here*.

Martin peeks out the window and points at the men around the log, three to each side, everyone can see them eying the library door. Beneda raises her bow and looses an arrow, Martin points once again, as Beneda looses two more, asking, "How do we get into Zenobia for a letter?"

"There is a coal chute," lowering the bow, she answers, "to the basement. On the east side." Looking back at Jolan, she keeps on, "Could be climbed into. A small enough person could get through that."

"I do it." Jolan pipes up, "I climb *real* good!"

Caleb adds an, "Uh-huh, he do!"

"It'll be more wiggling than climbing, you up for that?" Asante reaches for him and Jolan nods so fast, his head wobbles under the scout's hand, his eyes meet hers. "I'll go with him. That's where Willy was setting the traps."

"Hey," Miss Bessie says, coming in with some clumping steps. "I brung sandwiches an fruit, an carrots. You'all need to eat." She lifts the big bag and holds onto her side like the stairs were too much.

Missus Washington grabs it from her, telling Caleb. "Well, we gots a job for you now. You be the runner up and down these here stairs for Miss Bessie, hear?"

Jolan and Caleb run over and grab food, glad to both be a part of this, for sure. *Poor Bessie*, the walk here has taken most of the day.

"What about him?" Pete with a sandwich in his hand, points his sword at the prisoner.

"Best take him to the sheriff to be locked up." Asante waves toward town. "Tell the sheriff that the library will bring charges."

"I'ma coming. I want a word with that so-called sheriff." Old Lady stands, only wobbles a bit. But her voice is strong, even after that long walk.

"I can interview him, don't you think?" The reporter asks, "About why he isn't doing more?"

There is what Jolan hears as a general agreement at that notion. As they gather around the prisoner, Beneda turns to the window and commences loosing more arrows.

27 Captured - Trickster

They still weren't inside. *This ain't right,* Cootuh fumes. *This be take'n too long. Malcolm and his group here at the back door been tryin' for almost two days.* The fire still burns, but they've given up with the lit arrows. What with that girl up there; always stomping them out.

Loud cussing and moaning comes as a man staggers back to Cootuh's knot of men, an arrow sticking out of his shoulder. Sweat plasters the man's shirt to his skin. *Another one!*

Hissing in frustration Cootuh looks over the wall of wooden slats Sam's people are trying to build. A decent wall could protect them from Beneda's cursed arrows. But, they haven't got any decent material to work with. Cootuh's hat whips against his leg, and not for the first time today.

He pats Nick, the young archer trying to patch up the wounded. No medical supplies and no one trained in doctoring. Kevin yells for help as he comes around the far corner of the library, herding some women and a boy.

"Look who we done caught, Mister Cootuh!" he brags. Kevin's arm is bandaged, but swings free. "I got my sword back." With that he shoves the boy forward.

Frowning, Cootuh stops and both hands go to pushing his hat back on, “What you got there?”

Smiling and waving his sword again, Kevin boasts, “We caught ’em coming back to that building across the way. They’s lots of folk come now. Gots swords, clubs, and staffs.”

“Why’d you grab them?”

“This ‘un had my sword.” He holds out the hilt, showing a dark cord wrapped around the hand guard.

“Well ladies…, sir.” Cootuh ducks his head at them, willing a smile to his lips. “I hope this unpleasantness will be over soon. Soon as Beneda stops those damned arrows.”

The old woman scowls at him, cursing. “She drive one through yo black heart. Her grandma teach her, more’n good enough.”

Cootuh’s happy for a distraction from the angry old lady, as he spies Malcolm coming around to vex him.

“We broke into the side room.” Malcolm shakes his head, seeing the newcomers. It stops him for a second. “We still can’t get into the main library. They’ve barricaded the inner door.”

Cootuh rubs his head. So tired. Can’t think clearly. “We’ll try the front again.” he finally decides.

For once Malcolm offers no snide remark, “I’m worried we need to end this soon.”

“You right to worry,” The old lady snaps. The prisoners gaze intently at the two of them.

Cootuh surprises himself and Malcolm, putting a hand on his shoulder and turning them to face away toward the woods, whispering, “Beneda’s people won’t just wait us out. They’ll be sending for help. Sheriffs, marshals, somebody. We can’t stay much longer."

"You hear from Octavia?"

"She sent a rider. She's about ten kilometers away. Moving slow."

Malcolm, gives a glance back, eying the prisoners. "They know Beneda?"

Cootuh nods, but calls to the young bowman, "Nick. Take these three over to the big tree and stand a watch, so they don't escape." *Don't want Malcolm to get any crazy ideas.*

As the young man leads the three a few meters away, Malcolm's eyes track them. He ponders, "Can we use them to force that archer girl to give herself up?"

Thinking about that angry old lady, Cootuh gives that a second, and shakes his head, *no*. "Don't think so. But, I'll see what I can get out of them." His mind says, *Put Malcolm off. Get a few minutes to think.* "If we can just destroy those papers, we can leave the girl to her damn arrows." His hand is still on Malcolm's shoulder, "How bout you try for an idea— how to lure the librarians out. You good at that."

"Okay." Malcolm's eyes pierce Cootuh, *probably losing trust. Well, as long as Octavia's not here yet…*

Cootuh's mind frantically tries for a clearer thought about how to end this resistance. And he shoves at nothing with his hands, till Malcolm grunts, but heads back around to his men back at the door.

Stepping over to the prisoners, he remembers Beneda's stubbornness.

"I want your help," addressing the grey haired woman, he squats and immediately regrets it. Ignores the well-dressed one, and the boy. Ignores his aching knee as well.

"Ain't getting spit from us."

The other, very calm and collected speaks up, "Mister Cootuh, I'm a reporter. For the Beaufort Gullah Times. I've been interviewing these two and would like to take them out of harm's way to continue my story."

"No, Ma'am." Cootuh tries thinking through the fog. "We can't have any newspaper articles. 'Til it's over."

"But—"

Cootuh stops her with a raised hand, *why can't I think?* "—Help me end this," he forces a smile on his weary face, "and you are all free to go."

"I'll tell you how to end it." The old woman utters, pulling fiercely tight at her knitted shawl. "You go now. It ended!"

Shaking his head, he's about to answer, but still another man runs up.

Sweating and nervous, this one, Sam, blurts, "Two men injured. They's traps on the North side. One's foot punctured. De other's bit. A rattler!"

Taking a deep breath, and cursing all hired bandits, he breathes, "Okay. That's alright." Got to calm this one down. "We take care of dem. What size de snake?"

His hands twitching, Sam spread them not quite the width of his stomach, and answers, "Little dark thing. Didn't hear rattlin' 'til we right up on it. They's a dozen o' them, put in a pit!"

Patting the air in front of the agitated young man, Cootuh calls over, "Jeremiah! Go with Sam. Bring the injured back. Don't worry, those pygmy rattlers ain't killers."

Turning back to the prisoners he sees a sly smile on the old woman's face. He imagines she's brung them rattlers in that silly knitted purse of hers.

~~~

Cootuh staggers, unsteady on his feet, after the long ride to meet up with Octavia, a hard ten kilometers away near Hardeeville. Resentful at finding her in camp eating lunch. *Just as well.* She'd only complicate the problems back here.

Coming back to the siege, the only thing that's cheered him is that his round trip, to the northwest, saved his hide from risking Beneda's arrows. And now after the long ride back, he faces all he's created behind the Library.

In just his two-hour absence, his camp looks like a hospital. Injured men everywhere. Snakesbites and spent arrows at every turn. Jeremiah comes up with a worried look. *Oh no!*

Hesitating, he doesn't seem like he wants to speak. Cootuh tries looking pleasant, and gestures to him. "Spill it boy, what is it?"

"Nick run off." Pausing a second. "An a prisoner." *I shoulda just kept to the horse and gone right past this damned place.* Quickly snapping his head over. *Yep.* Only two women now.

"When dis happen?" Soon's he say it, he thinks, *it don't matter*.

"Maybe an hour ago. I sent men after 'em." Pointing at the old woman. "Old Lady Harris, she constantly after me to turn a'gin you."

Drawing an angry frustrated breath, Cootuh slaps his sweaty hat against his thigh, watches the dampness
~~~

fly from it, and answers, “Let me talk to her.”

As he moves, he makes a decision. Speaking softly to Jeremiah. “Maybe we can use them to bring the librarians out.” Jeremiah walks closer. “That girl still on the roof with that silly hat?” Cootuh asks.

“Yep.” Jeremiah nods. Vigorously. *Frustrated too.* All those lost arrows.

“When I take them to the side of the building get that girl’s attention up here. You catch her eye; you point her to me. Mebbe my message will mean something.” He slaps his hat back on his head.

28 Roof - Heart

Lakisha runs down the steps. Excited by what she has to tell Zenobia. The smell of fire is stronger down here. The attackers must be burning books in the room they've broken into off to the right wing.

She finds Zenobia standing at an inner door to the seized room with Preston. There she stops beside the big barricade of books and rocks they have set there, blocking its doorway.

"Zenobia!" Lakisha gasps for breath, she holds her side and stops for breath. "Two women are being held on the east side of the building!"

"Who?"

"The farmer woman… Old Lady. An the reporter woman, from Beaufort." Lakisha knows she knows the name, but can't think, there's a sharp stitch from running downstairs from the roof so fast.

"What they want?" Preston asks.

"The bad man, he was signaling, pointed to the front. So I ran there and looked. They cleared out. All a them, away from the front door."

As Zenobia thinks on this, Preston brings a cup of water to Lakisha. Thanking him with her eyes she takes a drink. She takes off the hot, sweat-filled helmet.

Zenobia orders, "Preston. Bring me one of the

Librarian's official robes, from Oliver's office!" As he hurries off, she tells the girl, "They want to get me out that door."

"But. They bad."

"Yes, well I'm not worried." Preston rushes back with a long flowing, brightly colored robe. He helps Zenobia into it. "They won't harm a Librarian. They know what *that* would mean for them."

Preston asks, "What should we do?"

"Lock the door behind me." Comes her reply. "The papers they want are in a locked safe. None of us have the combination." Patting Lakisha, the librarian tells her, "Climb up there."

Lakisha takes some breaths and climbs up on the bookcase, "Check no one is by the door." She peers out a small hole they had made to view attackers. Seeing nothing she waves to Zenobia.

Zenobia stands erect and opens the door. After she steps out, Preston locks it tight.

~~~

Back on the roof, Lakisha's hair is sticky and plasters the side of her face. *Helmet's be horrible. I ain't never wear one after today.* Looking over the roof's façade she spies Zenobia, walking slowly to the south corner of the Library, to the women and the plainly dressed man with them.

That Cootuh, she thinks, though she can't rightly see his face under that hat.

He bows low to Zenobia as she stops, out of reach, a few feet from him. Her shadow barely darkens his shoes. *Wonder if he fooled by the robe?*

Cootuh waves the women over. Zenobia hugs each of them, one under each outstretched arm. They
~~~

commence to walk back toward the library's front door. Lakisha shouts down, "Man coming!" when she notices someone running, coming along from the back of the library.

Zenobia glances up first. Worry in her face. Seeing Lakisha pointing, the librarian puts a hand on each woman's back to push them faster. She turns, stops and faces the approaching man.

Frantically Lakisha tries to think of something to do. Her eyes keep snapping between Zenobia and the surrounding forest. Noticing a flash of light in a small clearing toward the stream. *Asante!* Then he disappears and she sees only Aza in the green space.

Yelling, she waves her arms, "Aza!" When the dog looks up and starts in yapping, she motions rapidly, straight down to where the man has grabbed Zenobia's arm. "Help!"

In the next second Aza can't be seen any longer. Looking back down Lakisha watches two more men coming up behind Cootuh. One with a club, the other a sword.

She feels like crying. *What can I do?* Almost too fast to see, Aza's dark form flashes from the woods and with a huge leap he smashes into the chest of the man grabbing hold of Zenobia. Lakisha falls to her stomach and watches all below.

Falling down, the man has put up his hands to hold back the snarling dog. Lakisha has to hang her head over to see where he's fallen. Zenobia is quickly backing away to the front of the library.

The swordsman runs up and raises his sword over Aza. A shout pulls her eyes back to the trees. Asante races out with his sword. *Now they'll get what Stick did!* A meter behind him three more men come out of the trees, hope rises in Lakisha's heart, *Get em!* Cootuh's men start backing away, not expecting any of this.

With Aza safe, Lakisha leans farther over the front of the building to find Zenobia, dizzying herself, the helmet nearly falling on the ruckus below. Just as she strains, the front door slams closed.

29 Army - Soul

Jolan sits just outside the door scrubbing his feet, hearing the adults speaking inside the room. Missus Porter, Mister Martin's daughter, said Jolan needs to be cleaned up to be in her home, so he's doing his best with his feet as they talk.

From inside, Jolan can hear the questions fly, "Dad, you've rode how far?"

First the long ride from Bluffton. Now washin'… Jolan's rear is sore from their hurried ride. Then waiting at the gate for an hour. *I'm tired!* The soldiers had kept the gate closed all that time. Finally, they sent a message to Captain Porter and he came and led them here to his wife, Carrie.

Now I gots to do these. Cleaned em up plenty. Jolan examines that living room as he dries his toes there on the front porch. Missus Porter gave him a big bucket and towels. It's a small house. Everything spotless. Flower patterns on window curtains. He drops the scrub brush into the bucket, and wipes his hands on his backside.

"Thank you, Carrie." Mister Martin is saying. *He eating cornbread, didn't have to wash his feet afore comin in.* "Appreciate you takin' us in. And we appreciate your husband for advocate'n for us farmers."

"I'm sure John will do the right thing. Relieving a siege is in their experience, I'm sure." Giving her father a smile, she's also snatched up the towel she's given Jolan, folding it into a damp tidy square. "And, his commander likes him, right now."

"How come?"

"Superior officers were down two weeks ago." She holds a second. "Carrying out an inspection. They especially were impressed with John's company. He's strict but fair."

"Good. Hope we can leave soon. I worry about the others we left behind."

Looking over at Jolan, she tells him, "I might have some sandals that will fit you. Let me look." Jolan hardly hears, heading for the cornbread the way he does.

"Don't want no women's shoes." He whispers, once his mouth's full.

"Hush, Jolan. You'll take what my daughter give you. Or, I'll tell Missus Washington you acting up."

"Ah now…" Jolan wants to protest, but the front door opens and Captain Porter in his uniform enters. Jolan's swallow of bread sticks for a moment, in awe, as the captain had taken time to change into a fancier uniform before going to ask for help.

"Captain." Both Martin and Jolan jump up.

Nodding, Captain Porter takes off his gold braided hat. "Well, Sir, you got what you came for." Mister Martin lets out a large breath. "My commander's heard your tale, he's given permission for me to take a platoon to relieve Bluffton."

Mister Martin wrings his hands. "How soon can we leave?" Jolan grabs up two more slabs of cornbread, stuffing them into his shirt.

"First thing in the morning."

"Why so slow?"

At Martin's frown, the Captain holds up his hand. "They are readying a ship for us. We can be there in hours. Tomorrow."

Missus Porter comes back in, sandals in her small hand. "Honey? Good news?" at his nod, she turns to Jolan. "Here. Should fit you."

Taking them, Jolan examines them. *Ain't girly t'all!* He tries one. Then the other. *They fit!*

"The ship's being outfitted and loaded." Porter steps over to Jolan, looking down at the boy. "We got a problem. Would you be willing to help, young fellow?"

Jolan jumps up from the floor, with his new sandals cinched snug. "Yes, Sir!"

"All our full time pigeon handlers are on leave." Shakes his head from his great height. *Must be some fix he in!* The Captain says to Mister Martin, "We use the pigeons to communicate with headquarters." Back to Jolan he asks, "Would you be willing to work with them?"

"Yay. I cain't wait!" He gives his best salute.

The Captain nods. "Alright. Mister Martin, I'll see you later. Carrie, don't wait supper. I'll be with the troops most of the night. Come with me, soldier."

His wife comes gives him a hug and kiss. Jolan's set, pats at his shirt. *Pigeons love 'em cornbread crumbs.*

Captain Porter waves a new officer over. "Jolan, this is Private Billy Aesop. He's a trainee with the pigeon messenger service. He'll supervise you. Do whatever he shows you. Understood?"

Jolan stands straight and executes a second sharp salute. "Yes, sir." With a smile the captain walks away.

"You ready to learn about pigeons?" the young officer asks.

"'kay! I mean. Yes, sir!" His trek forgotten, and his belly full, Jolan is feeling full of energy again.

With a laugh, Aesop shakes the boy's hand, "No need for all the parade dress, I'm a private just like you, son."

Opening the door to the building, Private Aesop leads him in. A soft cooing noise fills the space. "This is the loft." Jolan's eyes go wide at the rows and rows of boxes filling the room. Cooing rises in the air. The backs of Jolan's arms feel prickly, like he's been here once in a dream.

"How many birds here?"

"Over one hundred." Moving to the side, explaining about the boxes, and groups of birds they'll be using. "We will take ten pigeons tomorrow."

"What's I suppose to do?"

"Our most important job is to keep the pigeons comfortable and calm." Pointing to some boxes near the door, Jolan can hear the clicks and shuffles. "It's important that they not be afraid. This one's Simon."

Opening a box, he holds Jolan's hand inside. He feels the bird's feathers as it moves around. "Oh." It's soft.

"Handle them gently. They need to smell us and be calm with us." Private Aesop shows Jolan about feeding and cleaning up the birds.

When they step outside, Jolan's surprised how much time has passed. "It's *dark!*"

~~~
~~~

The ship's still tied to the dock. Jolan's nose is full of salt air. Jolan was sleepy an hour ago, when the Captain's wife woke him. Then it was dark outside. Now the sun is beginning to rise across the ocean. The ribbon of bone white lays low on the waves, a pinkish glow rising up from that, chasing the darkness up and up.

Jolan and Private Aesop have squeezed into a tight space beside the rail, with their birds in boxes. Men are running back and forth on the wooden deck.

"How many men are here?" Jolan wants to know.

"The Eagle usually carries about fifty sailors to work her."

"Dang!" Jolan's eyes tail up to the ship's three masts. "This here be a big ship."

Smiling, Private Aesop says, "No, the *Eagle*'s called a schooner. Only 90 meters long."

Seems big to Jolan. He stares at the three long poles jutting into the sky, covered with men climbing like monkeys.

"We goin' now?"

The private points to a woman near Martin's son-in-law. "The captain will decide."

The woman, with grey streaked hair poking out, trying to escape from her cap, stands beside Captain Porter.

She shouts, "Set sail stations!" Around the ship her call is repeated by others.

"Now's the time, sir," She informs Captain Porter. "Tide'll be against us if we don't sail now."

"Very well. My men are set." Captain Porter answers with a quick bow. Jolan looks across to where Mister Martin huddles with the rest of the soldiers on the far end of deck. Seems like more that twenty men with long spears and short swords.

"Why they swords so small?" He turns back to Aesop, he should know. "They ain't much bigger 'an Bowie knives."

"This platoon belongs to a pike company." The private explains. "Pikes are the main weapon, those long spears. The sword is a backup in case of a melee."

The captain, she hurries off, shouting her orders. Jolan looks at the dock as the lines are thrown off, on the pier men wrap the thick ropes around bollards. Loud snapping noises turn his eyes up as the once empty masts fill with white sails.

As the ship rocks under them, Private Aesop announces, "The tide is taking us."

We come'n Beneda.

30 Safe Library - Warrior

Fields are burning. Children are crying. Her arm is being tugged.

"'Neda!" Marquetta, her friend's voice. "Wake up."

Opening her eyes, Beneda looks blearily around. *The classroom.* She sits on the floor, leaning against a bag. *Across from the library.* "I'm up," she mumbles.

It takes a second, but then it hits, Marquetta eyes radiate pain, that look scares her, no one's gotten hurt so far. *What could this news be?* "Pete's back."

Rising, Beneda reaches for her bow. "What's wrong? Sally! Sally, wake up child!"

Sniffing, Marquetta tells her, "Pete. He hurt. An' Old Lady been captured."

"No!" Beneda actually stops moving. Shocked. Then, "I'm going."

"Slow down." Marquetta grabs her arm. "Yo mama say you need to plan what we do."

"I'ma see Pete. You wake that girl. She's my eyes, damn it all."

"He asleep now. Down in the kitchen, near them ovens. That doctor the reporter woman sent for from Beaufort, he say Pete need his rest."

Trying to calm herself, Beneda thinks. With some deep breaths, she decides, "Okay." She casts a serious look on Marquetta, she'll get all the news soon enough. "Have the leaders up come here. I'll talk to them."

As Marquetta moves to head back downstairs, Beneda moves to Sally. The girl slumbers on the floor with a blanket over her thin shoulders. Shaking her arm gently, Beneda thanks her luck, having a spotter with such good eyes.

The sleepy girl looks up with a start. "Sally. Time to go back to work, child."

Nocking an arrow, Beneda scans the front of the library.

"Look like dey gave up on de battering ram." Sally, her chin on the window sill, comments.

Beneda's arm aches. Loosing arrows all through the night kept the enemy's heads down. But, now she pays for it with an arm and fingers that throb every time she moves. Beneda plans as she looks out the window. "Sally. Go fetch Eathan. Let's use him up here."

Nodding, Sally heads to the door. Looking at the pile of arrows near the window, Beneda thinks, *wish we had more*. Eathan will do just fine, a young farmer with a bow. *Not as accurate as me.*

From the hall she hears steps and voices coming. Another glance out the window, then Beneda concentrates on what to tell the others.

Her mama comes in and moves quickly over to Beneda for a hug. Young Turner clumps in behind her, with Mister Hogg and Marquetta following.

"Beneda." Turner greets her.

Another deep breath. "I am running out of arrows." Letting that sink in. "We need to drive them away from that library door. Now."

Mister Hogg just stares into Beneda's eyes. Turner grinds his teeth. "So we can fetch some back." Giving an approving nod. Mama's lips turn into a frown, pale around the edges. *They've come to trust me.* Beneda tries to keep from choking up, refusing to look into Marquetta's face.

"I've sent for Eathan to come take over, here." Composing herself. "I'll lead everyone we have can fight. Out there."

"But…" Mama speaks up. Beneda raises a hand to stop her.

Like a flash, Aza trots into the room, looks around for a minute then sets at attention. Everyone's eyes glue to the doorway. Beneda's heard nothing. Silently, Asante moves into the room. Taking in Beneda, he steps over, and in front of the others gathers her into his arms. Neither willing to release the other.

Now tears come to her eyes, she whispers into Asante's shoulder, "They captured Old Lady, and h… hurt Pete," she stumbles out.

He gives her a small smile, holds her by her chin and raises it up a bit. "Old Lady is okay." Waving out the window. "She's safe in the Library."

Exhaling in relief, Beneda hugs him again, then pushes back.

"I decided we need to drive Cootuh's men back." She points across the way.

Asante gazes out at those men crouched near the library door for a moment. Then nods, as he glances at her small pile of remaining arrows.

~~~

Beneda's focus hangs on a slender thread. She
~~~

can't stop worrying. *Wish Old Willy were here to help. Need to make a list. Save the library, protect the innocent, save the farms, keep Asante*.

"Eathan and Sally are keeping eyes on us," she tells Mama. They stand with a crowd beside the school. "We'll start the attack from back here. Cootuh's people won't see us."

Her mama looks her over. "You ready? Don't have many arrows." Running her hands over the fletching on the five in Beneda's quiver.

"I'll have more, once we reach the library." She tries once again, gives a serious look, and asks, "Mama. You sure you want to do this? We gots enough fighters."

"I doing it for the farm, and the children." Pointing to the school. "All ones in der. With Bessie, Eathan, Sally, an dat new archer."

"Thanks mama." She waves over to Turner. "Your group is there." A last hug. Her eyes follow her mother's back. "Love you."

Trying not to worry for a moment, reassuring herself about Bessie keeping the children organized and busy, Beneda listens to the sounds of birds. First ones she's noticed in two days. *Good omen.* She smiles at the sight of Marquetta coming down the school's steps.

"Pete awake."

"Good." A pair of earrings registers with Beneda as she gazes at her best friend.

Seeing Beneda notice, Marquetta brushes one. It dangles and sways there. "From Pete."

Gulping, keeping her face still, Beneda finds it hard to put a smile on her face, yet she does. "They look good!" The black pearls are smaller than she remembers and the thin strip of gold shines in the morning light.

Marquetta snorts. "Decided he wants to call on me. Mebbe walk out wif me when all this done." With a smile. "I been tend'n to him so well."

Beneda forces a little laugh, covering her thoughts. "Good for you." Seeing the club in Marquetta's hand. "You in my group?"

"Yeah." A frown crosses Marquetta's face. She forgets Pete's trinkets and points over across the way. "You sure about this? Fight'n armed men?"

"Don't see no choice." Shaking her head slowly, Beneda watches Asante and the others in their places now. Marquetta nods, willing even if having doubts. "We need arrows. And can't let them take the library."

Asante raises his sword high, the score of folk fall quiet. Slowly and silently he examines the faces before him. Their feet shuffle, but, they wait for him, ready with their attention.

"Today's actions build the future." Then he pauses. "The Zulu warriors attacked in formations shaped like buffalo horns." Holding his hands beside his head. "Each horn thrusts against the sides of the enemy. Then the chest comes up the middle." He pantomimes, and heads nod. There's little grumbling. *Ready as they'll ever be.* "Beneda and I will lead each horn."

Beneda thinks about trust, then takes over. "Turner will lead all remaining folks up the center. We experienced fighters be on the sides, we'll take on protecting those headed for the door." Pausing and taking a breath before continuing, *be the horn*, she recites, "Pick up every arrow you come across! If we don't beat 'em back beside and behind the library, then we fall back to the front door. Hold it till Martin comes with help."

Looking at the small groups, she understands Marquetta's worry. *Only five people in my horn.* At least Hector looks fierce. Bulging muscles and a big club. She lists in her head, *Another five with Asante. Please let this be the right decision.*

"We do this for our farms. And the children," Mama Washington says once more.

31 Library Fight - Trickster

Cootuh stands beside his command tree, frustration simmering. *A simple job,* he'd told them all, *break into this here building. We go in through the back, nobody even the wiser.* He has a clear view of the men still standing, and the back of the library with that blessed door. None able to breach the place as of yet, and too many down with arrow wounds. Everyone knows where to find him, though few risk bringing him anymore bad news. He observes Jeremiah rushing over.

"Octavia's men are here! Malcolm, he already gather'n up."

"Finally." *Sick of looking at the back of this place.* "Where's *she* be?"

"By the creek." Jeremiah reports, pointing. "Brung shields made to protect 'gainst dem arrows."

Looking at the early morning light filtering through the trees, Cootuh grumbles, "Now we can end this. We done spent three days too long camped here. Someone's coming to stop us, sure."

Jeremiah winces at that thought, stands a bit straighter, he tilts his head at the newer men back here, a worried look as he asks, "What *we* do?"

Wiping sweat from his brow, thinking, "Have Sam organize the extra men to join Malcolm. And get the shields." Waving to the creek, Cootuh explains. "I'm fin'ta see to Octavia. You on your own for a tick."

Several long minutes later, stepping out of the woods onto the creek bank, Cootuh spies Octavia, perched on a camp chair, a glass in her hand. *Where'd she get ice?*

Noticing, she waves him over, demanding, "What's happening?"

Cootuh stops to think what's most important. *Get everyone away from Bluffton.* "We're about to break in. Thanks for bringing the extra men. And them shields. Good idea."

She smiles up at him. Perfect hair and not a speck of dirt on her riding habit. "I should be there."

Shaking his head firmly. "No, Miss." *and it comes to him,* "You might be recognized." *Go ahead and make that face, girl, I got my orders too.* "It'll all be over today. Head on back to the big house. Malcolm and I can join you there."

Pouting, she says, "But, I want to see something. I traveled all this way."

Struggling to freeze a smile on his face, Cootuh answers like she's a slow child, teeth showing a goodwill he definitely does not feel. "Authorities will be here soon. Anyone who can be identified will be arrested."

She examines his expression. He breathes though his nose, waiting. Finally, Octavia gives a small nod. "If I must. I will have the men take me back."

Now, Cootuh smiles for real. "Yes, Miss. Like I say, it be over today. We be back soon."

As he returns to the library, shouting reaches Cootuh through the thinning trees. Breaking into a run, he wonders, *Darn it, now what?* Reaching the clearing where he can see the back façade, he's faced with swirling confusion. He whistles loud and piercing, standing at what he calls his *Command Tree.* Men are running or limping from the sides of the library and disappearing into the woods left and right. Cootuh yells at them, "Men! Stop!" But he's ignored.

Trying to listen over the many sets of thudding boots, and see through the kicked up dust, Cootuh can't make out what's going on near the front of the building. A last, he sees Jeremiah running.

"They're attack'n!" Jeremiah blurts.

Cootuh gets lucky, and manages to grab his shoulder, nearly lifting the young man off his feet. "Who?"

"Farmers!" As Jeremiah wiggles and tries catching his breath, Cootuh has a vision of a few farm kids, bare feet, waving play weapons; branches and reeds.

"How many?" He grins.

"Couldn't see." Jeremiah stops talking, just gasps now, from his run. Then his eyes focus on Cootuh, and he remembers himself for a moment. "Not many…"

"Help me grab some of these fools." Cootuh waves around at the confused, fleeing men. "You grab two and hold them! Any two!"

Cootuh darts and grabs one to the left, then another by his sleeve. They tug mightily, but he drags them back to where Jeremiah stands holding his two men.

"Stop!" Cootuh yells. He shakes the one who

wiggles the most. “This be easy. We just fight a minute. We win. Okay?”

His two calm down. In the two that Jeremiah’s holds, Cootuh sees wildness, white around too much of those dark eyes, but they’ve given up trying to run.

“Good. Now pick up weapons.” He points out of the tree line where the recruits have been dragged. Of the four, only one still clutches a club. But the clearing is littered with dropped cudgels and knives. Cootuh’s worried but finally releases the two he’s has hold of.

Jeremiah has freed his and stepped back to block their escape route. *Good idea.* Cootuh sidles over, blocking and guiding his two to where Jeremiah stands.

“Now.” He looks each one in the eye, and points back to the clearing. “We’re going back to the front. Follow me.” He thinks on that, then orders, “No. You head out first. Till we out of these woods. Stay together. We’ll be safe together.”

Nodding to Jeremiah to bring up the rear, Cootuh trots at their left, through the last of the woods, and back onto the field of battle, *such as it is*.

~~~

Cootuh spots two people coming his way as he moves around the building. *Beneda!* Beside her strides Hector with a huge club.

Cootuh freezes and waves his two men forward. Jeremiah, stopping also, pushes his two toward *Hector*. Cootuh moves closer to the wall on his left. *Maybe, if I duck right quick, the wall’ll stop that club.*

As Hector swings wildly, Beneda’s raised her bow. In an instant Cootuh’s looking at a arrowtip
~~~

aimed his way.

As she releases, Malcolm smashes into her from behind. The arrow plants in the ground, inches from Cootuh's boot.

A man bounces from the wall in front of Cootuh's men. *Damn!* Looking over he realizes Hector's alone, except for this one hanging on his back. Jeremiah's eyes meet his. "There!" Cootuh commands.

On trembling legs, Jeremiah steps in front of Hector. But he only blocks the huge man for a second. That club crashes down on his shoulder and Jeremiah drops like a felled tree. Out cold.

Hector flings the last man off his back. Off and away. "Wait!" Cootuh shouts. It works, Hector freezes with club raised.

There's movement and grunting, out of the corner of his eye, Cootuh notices Malcolm on top of Beneda. Sees both her hands grip his wrist. Malcolm's small knife close to her face. With the free hand he hits the girl's head and chest.

"Hector. We friends." Cootuh's spread his hands apart, eyes opened as wide as they'll go.

Shaking his head and the club, Hector growls, "No."

"You worked for me." Cootuh forces a distorted smile. "The farmers killed Brutha." Cootuh casts his face toward Beneda as she struggles. Cootuh's thinking the knife in his hand is a twin to Malcolm's but his won't stop Hector.

"No!" With Hector's shout comes a jolt of pain in Cootuh's hand. Hector's club has smashed down.

As Cootuh backs away, another black shape comes moving rapidly toward the struggling pair on the ground.

"Malcolm!" His shout too late. The old attacker has thrust a Bowie knife into Malcolm's kidney. *That old man, what helped the scout and the librarian woman.* Now Hector's closer.

Careful where he steps, *No mora this!* Cootuh's turned now, *Feets!* Not caring to see or hear more, he tilts full speed, heading to the creek.

32 Sandals - Heart

A soldier passes, leading a prisoner, as Lakisha admires her new sandals. She breathes deep the fresh air outside on the library's porch. *Directing little boys is hard.*

Caleb runs out from between the library's strong columns, calling, "Jolan hit me."

In an instant Jolan rushes out on his trail. "He called my sandals girly!"

"'Cause. Look at my feets!" Caleb holds up a foot covered with black soot from working to clear the burned books.

"Caleb." Lakisha scolds. "Leave Jolan alone. We look into something for you feet later. Okay?"

Caleb seems to consider, a mulish look on his face, before he blurts, "An' Jolan gots pigeon poop on 'em!"

Seeing Jolan raising his fist to strike, Lakisha shouts, "Jolan!" As he freezes, looking at her, she says softly, "You are Caleb's leader now. Do you know what that means?"

His big eyes stare. "No…"

"Just like Beneda led the farmers." Lakisha's face turns grave, she holds up an arrow she's found lodged under the bench and shakes it at the taller of the two boys. "You have to think about what *helps* Caleb. *You* have to help Caleb. Okay."

Slowly his hand falls. "Yas'um."

Nodding strictly to them both. "Good. Now git back to work. You know what to do?"

Jolan looks to Caleb, letting him speak. "We's pile up good books on one side. Hurt books on de other."

"Right. Now go." She waves down to the picnic basket on the grass. "We eat in fifteen minutes."

"Yay!" The boys shout and run back in, sandals forgotten that quickly.

Feeling a warm soft form rubbing her leg, she looks down, at Aza and his wiggly tail. As she lowers her hand, his wet nose nuzzles her palm.

Asante smiles down at her and Aza. "I see you put those boys to work."

"Yes. There be damage in the room dey bandits got into. Big job." Pointing at some soldiers, Lakisha asks. "What dey doing with the bad 'uns?"

Asante waves to town. "They've taken over a horse corral to hold all prisoners. Marshalls are coming to organize a trial."

"Hope they get what coming to dem."

"Are you staying?" Asante asks, nodding at the building.

"Yes! Zenobia says I can help at the front desk. And, the kitchen."

"Congratulations." The scout touches her shoulder, nodding his head. Aza rests on his haunches and seems happy, as well. "You earned it."

The opening door catches their attention. So much to do, so much to set right again. Zenobia, in plainer robes now, steps onto the porch.

"You had to return the Librarian's robes?" Asante

asks with a wry smile.

"I am being punished." Her head tilts with a crooked smile of her own. "For signing the Librarian's name to fetch the military to us." Lakisha thinks, *There's a joke there, I bet.*

"You saved lives." Asante tells her, without a laugh or smile.

"Yes. One of my lesser crimes." Now Zenobia's smile looks happier at his words. "Librarian Oliver's been transferred." Extending a finger toward the building. "Librarian Lincoln will oversee here and audit what happened."

Reaching into his bag, Asante pulls out a book. "Beneda bade me return this book to you. Now the danger is ended."

Considering it for a long moment, Zenobia finally takes it in her hands. "Please express to Beneda how grateful we are to her." Looking down at the book. "This will have a place of honor in our library, and she and her family will have access to it at all times."

Asante bows formally at her words.

With a shout, the boys scamper back out of front door. "Aza!" the pup gives them a bark as they halt in front of him, and fall to their knees for some petting and patting.

"It fifteen minutes?" Jolan asks expectantly.

Nodding Lakisha scoots over to the basket and hands out sandwiches. The boys plop down on the grass before the wide columns of the Library, and wiggle their toes. Aza stretched out at their feet, keeps his eyes on their hands and mouths.

Zenobia lowers her voice when she touches Asante's shoulder, "When you get a chance. Librarian Lincoln asks to speak with you."

"Yes. I will see her now." Looking down to his guide, he pauses to ask Lakisha. "Are you going to be able to get everything done?"

"Oh, yes!" Lakisha clacks her heels together and the new sandals Zenobia's gifted her make a very satisfying sound. "Preston is going to bide a while. And Mama bringing Peanut to stay with me."

"Excellent. We shall talk again." Next he orders, "Aza. Wait here. Keep these boys safe, now." Lakisha *gets* that joke.

~~~

Lakisha notices Jolan trying not to rock too much. All the adults stand around him talking in the big meeting room. Librarian Lincoln is here, speaking with Captain Porter and Missus Washington. Lakisha catches Jolan's fingers running over the spine of a book on the nearby shelf.

"I like it." Missus Washington says. "The Washington place will be happy to provide a location for the messenger birds."

Captain Porter nods. "Then it's agreed. Private Aesop will travel with several birds to your farm and setup a loft."

The Librarian reaches over to touch Jolan's arm. "Do you agree to work with the pigeons on your farm, young man?"

That stops the books being touched. With his eyes wide and shining, Jolan's head bobs vigorously. "Yas'um." He glances at Missus Washington who gives him a smile and a nod, *proud as he is*, Lakisha thinks. *Proud like me, with the job here now.*

Librarian Lincoln tells the boy, "You and Private Aesop will help us by doing this."
~~~

With a big grin, Jolan announces, “I get Caleb to help.” He looks to Lakisha, “Cuz, I his leader now.”

Lakisha covers her mouth, but can’t hide her delighted grin.

33 Home - Warrior

Savannah Chasseur squints at the temporary plaque, bolted to the left of the entry on one of the library's strong pillars. She reads aloud, "Thanks to the courageous action of Beneda Washington, and the farmers of Daufuskie Island in May, this year, the Bluffton Library was protected from attackers." Beneda is feeling more and more embarrassed as the words come, that voice clear and sure. The reporter's pencil stands poised. "What would you like to tell my readers."

"Oh, Savannah!"

Patting Beneda's shoulder, the reporter encourages, "You should be proud."

"I didn't do anything."

Savannah laughs, pretends to write a second, then reads, "Beneda of Washington Farm, says, she didn't do anything. The arrows shot themselves. The farmers mysteriously stood organized, and Cootuh's bandits magically found themselves defeated."

Beneda shakes her head in amusement. She can't stay angry at the older woman. "Don't write that silliness."

"Then don't speak it." Savannah strikes a pose. Holding her pencil in the air dramatically. "I represent the reporting of truth in this era we find ourselves in.

My readers depend on my honesty and nose for digging to get them the truth."

Shaking her head Beneda smiles, *no stopping this one.* "Are you headed home?"

"No. Old Lady Harris has invited me to visit her farm." Savannah smiles at personal memories. "We talked while trapped in the library."

"Another story?"

"Yes." Savannah gives a vigorous nod. She mimes a paper's headline, "The True Story of The Farms On Daufuskie Island."

Smiling Beneda thinks, *I can see why Old Lady wants to spend more time with her.* "Thank you for bringing us a doctor. He really helped Pete."

"I'm glad." Shaking her head. "But, this story has been good for my paper. Do you know, there has not been any other attack on a regional library in fifty years?"

"Really? Fifty?"

"Years ago, while their power grew, they'd have scouts and groups of guards to defend the books and Librarians." Savannah points up at the building. "It's been years since they've felt the need."

Beneda spies Old Willy shambling up, leading a horse. Several boxes lashed on its back.

"Willy." Beneda greets him.

"Beneda. I's takin' Jolan an' Caleb home."

Nodding, she grins, *those boys will have stories to tell for years.* She wants to express her gratitude. "Willy, thank you for—for my life."

With a smile Old Willy only shakes his head. "I grew up admiring yo M'Deah. I wish I could'a done more for her at the end." He gazes onto Beneda's face. *Perhaps*, she thinks, *seeing another.*

"You remind me so much a' her. I have to do for you, what I cain't do for her."

Beneda bites her lip, to avoid crying. *Gots to talk about something else.* She points, and asks, "What you got there?"

"Pigeons." He touches a box, Beneda notices how the reporter peeks in the little holes. Willy uses a gentle touch on it. She's sure Savannah's stored the scene for an article to come. "We be havin' a direct link wit the library. Jolan be workin' wit dem," He tells Missus Chasseur.

"Good." Beneda grins at thinking of the little one taking on this responsibility. "The farms have been isolated too long."

"I'll be off now. Ma'am" Willy's ducking his head to Savannah.

"I'll see you there." Giving him a bright smile, Savannah taps her pencil to her notebook. "I'm visiting the Harris Farm. Next one over?"

"That right. 'Til then." He touches his hand to his head, then pads down the road with the women watching.

In a moment, Beneda and Savannah are coughing from the dust of a crowd of people tramping up. Some walking and some on horseback.

Marquetta and Old Lady Harris come right up to the two women, as the others arrange themselves into a jumbled group.

"'Neda!" Marquetta squeaks out. "We going home."

"I see that, 'Quetta." Beneda laughs, *Girl still gots them earrings in*. "Don't breathe too much dust on the trip. And where's Pete."

"He staying a day or two." She doesn't seem

upset, sets a hand on those hips, and jabs a thumb behind her. "He help'n t' clean up."

Savannah announces, "I'm coming too. Let me grab my bag." She turns and runs into the library.

"When you coming, girl?" Old Lady asks Beneda.

"Just got to clean up some things." Beneda tries to keep sadness from her voice. "In a day or two."

"Well, you clean him up good." Marquetta winks and laughs, the horses shy and stamp at the sound.

As the group moves off, Savannah runs out and joins them, waving and blowing a good-bye to her new friend.

~~~

Beneda feels bad for the damage done to the school. It's a mess, and the students are back for classes. The farmers had dug holes and broken many branches on the bushes around the school building. Beneda'd offered to the headmistress, "We can get the farmers—to work on fixing things."

"No, Miss Beneda." The young woman shakes her head. Philippa was downstairs in a class when Beneda had come in to evacuate the children. "We're grateful to you, for keeping our little ones out of harm's way. Happy parents are going to make good all damages. You don't owe us anything. We owe you."

"Please—" with a smile and a shake, she pauses, remembers Asante's words. *Accept people's respect.* "—I am glad."

Pete speaks up, she'd nearly missed him coming in. "I bled in your kitchen." He strokes the bandage across his stomach.
~~~

Philippa waves it away. “Think nothing of the blood. It’s all cleaned up now.

They really do appreciate us, Beneda figures. “I’ll just go up to the classroom. See if we left anything.”

“Of course.” Philip waves upstairs. “The class is up there, but in another room.”

Climbing the stairs, Beneda reflects on how her life must return to normal. Listing what will come next: *Return to the farm, examine the fields, ready the next planting, say goodbye to Asante.*

Cain’t worry about the future, she tells herself, slowly moving up the stairs to let Pete keep up. He hobbles slowly.

“The doctor says I may never be able to run again.” Pete offers.

Beneda tries thinking what will help. “You doing all right with your walking.”

Pete gives an angry look at his leg. “I guess. I didn’t lose it.” A sigh. “I’m lucky.” He snaps a look her way. “Heard you was there when it happened. Years ago.”

Beneda knows he’s talking about Young Turner’s missing limb. “Yes. I saw the wagon roll over it.” She shudders at the memory. “What was left, looked awful.”

“Well, I guess, even he gets along fine now.” Pete lets out a separate sigh, for Young Turner.

Beneda’s glad Pete has accepted the fate he’s been given. She can mention the good, and does, smiling back at him there in the hallway, the sound of reciting from the far room up here. “Glad you and Marquetta’re get’n together.”

Pete bows his head. His shoulders fall a bit. “I

don' know what to say."

"Ain't nothing to say." She gives a bigger smile. "You both my friends. I happy for you both."

"Thanks, Beneda."

They walk into the abandoned room. Yes, it's a mess. But, Beneda doesn't see much left by the farmers. Sally's thin blanket. Some rags; when that wounded boy ran up here with the message. Bending down for the blanket she spies one arrow stuck under a chair. As she reaches, Beneda hears the clicking of nails in the hallway.

Aza. The pup trots over to her for a chance to lick her face. *The boys, and Lakisha will miss Aza so,* practicing the sound of Asante's *Yes,* in her head. Her eyes mist up as she stays crouched and rubs Aza's head. She decides she wants to convince the scout to let him stay.

Her head tilts up, *Well!* Asante steps into the room, in his librarian's vest, his hair trimmed, dressed for the road, she sees. Her hand remains on the pup. She doesn't rise. Doesn't want what may be said next.

"Beneda." He strides over. *Always so confident. I have to be that way, too.* So she rises, as he gives her a solid embrace.

Pete watches. His face slowly breaking into a smile. "Mister Asante. I want to thank you for helping us farmers."

"Of course. My duty is to the libraries and the people." He touches his chest. "I swore that oath, Pete, when I was made a scout."

Pete's focus moves then to Beneda. Without another word, he hobbles to the door and out. Only Pete's sigh lingers in the hallway.

Beneda thinks how to say her piece, *Be brave,*

say good-bye, no crying. "I will think of you as you travel on the Nairobi steam train."

"I don't want to go home. Now."

Beneda can't tell from his voice. *Should she have hope?* "What will you do?"

"I've spoken with Librarian Lincoln, about going after Cootuh."

That changes our talk. "Has Octavia Buckra been arrested?"

"No." Shaking his head ruefully. "Her father has. But, no one would, or could say they saw her do anything."

"So, she'll be running her father's plantation now?"

"It offends me, imagining the ones that avoided their punishment."

Beneda hides any sadness in her voice, "I was just imagining your journey home. On the way to Bungoma." She waves a hand to the window, her eyes away from his in this move. "I see the train running between the trees. And, along the African rivers." There's a wistful smile on his face that she catches, looking back to him. "In my mind, I was going to trace your route."

"I've been thinking about your life here." She ignores that. "I wonder what it will be like during the other seasons. Do the no-see-ums bother you in the fall and winter?"

Fond feelings for the land she loves bring a smile to Beneda. "Yes."

"I long to know how tall Jolan will grow." Asante stares out, thousands of miles into the distance. "I'd like to help him with his pigeons."

"Is that what you'd do after you catch Cootuh?"

Asante can't hide the grin, saying, "Possible. That, or come back here and try to find you."

"I'm sure, that a scout who can find the trickster, Cootuh, will be able to find me."

What to Read Next

Here are several titles you might be interested in, if you enjoyed this book.

Another book in the story of Library scouts is *Feeling a Way,* available in ebook and paperback. Another book in that series, *A Dangerous Way*, is available in Spanish, Italian and Esperanto translations.

Another series set in the same universe with an appearance by Library scouts two years earlier is titled The Protected Books. The first book in the series is *Pratima's Forbidden Book*, available in ebook, paperback, and hardcover.

Steerswoman by Rosemary Kirstein is a series about a young woman who has to travel through a primitive countryside to find the secrets about the world she lives in. Steerswomen are respected as keepers of the knowledge about the world.

Hellspark by Janet Kagan is about an investigator on a distant planet who solves crime and brings peace through her understanding of language, linguistics, body language and what drives people apart.

Satori by Dennis Schmidt is about a young swordsman who travels across the land and brings peace to a dangerous world.

Uplift War by David Brin is about several allies who are very different but who must work to survive on an alien planet.

The Hidden Queen by Alma Alexander is about a young girl who has to flee from those who would kill her and usurp her kingdom.

The Emperor's Edge by Lindsay Buroker is about a young woman who has to act to save the new emperor from the powers who would destroy him.

These Broken Stars by Amie Kaufman tells the story of a young man and young woman from different social classes who are stranded after a spaceship crash and must learn to work together to survive and uncover the secrets of the planet.

ABOUT THE AUTHOR

S A Gibson is a doctoral candidate in the field of education and has studied communication and computer science. He has lived in Northern and Southern California. His Facebook page is at ProtectedBooks.

ABOUT THE ARTISTS

Cover artwork in this book was originally hand drawn by Aaron Radney. Aaron is an Artist specialising in cover work and illustrations for books. His Facebook page is aradneyart.

The cover design and layout is by Rachel Bostwick. See her on Facebook at rachelbostwick and at rachelbostwick.com

Made in the USA
Columbia, SC
16 November 2020